A Seventh Child
A novel

John Strange Winter

Contents

A Seventh Child. A novel

BY

John Strange Winter

A SEVENTH CHILD

CHAPTER I.
WE ARE SEVEN.

Truth comes home to the mind so naturally, that when we learn it for the first time, it seems as though we did no more than recall it to our memory. —FONTENELLE.

From the world of spirits there descends A bridge of light connecting it with this, O'er whose unsteady floor that sways and bends, Wander our thoughts above the dark abyss. —**Haunted Houses.**

IT isn't all beer and skittles being the youngest of seven. Yes, I admit that "beer and skittles" is not the highest expression of social and linguistic art, but when you are the youngest of seven, and four of them are boys, you do get into a way of calling things by what boys always call their "right" names. I am the youngest of seven. Oddly enough my father was the youngest of seven and my mother was also the youngest of seven, so that I am the seventh child of a seventh child twice over. I need not say that my father's name was Septimus—Mother always called him Sep—and lucky it was that she was not called Septima. She was not, however, for her name was Blanche. We seven had neither hideous names like Septimus, nor ultra-fine names like Blanche. Madge was the eldest, and there was just ten years difference between her and me, so that when I was ten years old, Madge was twenty, and already engaged to be married.

As a matter of fact, she did not marry that man. Madge was excessively hand-some, and she was engaged several times before she finally married. Tom always said that it was because she was looking out for a better match than the man in possession, but I never thought Tom was right. It is true that I never understood why Madge engaged herself to James Allistair. He was not in any sense a proper or suitable match for her, being at least five-and-thirty, of no particular birth, of no especial position, and possessed of a shockingly bad temper and an exceedingly jealous disposition. Of course, at that time of day I was too young to realise all that I now know about James Allistair in looking back upon him.

I remember his coming one day to the old house on the outskirts of Manchester, which was the only home that I had ever known. I must have been ten years old then. He had walked out the half-mile from the town, where he lived, and as he came up the drive I was just crossing it from the shrubbery to the thicket. I don't know where the others were—I think they were all scattered about the place.

"Hullo, Nancy!" said he, "where is Madge?"

I don't know what made me say it, but I answered his thoughts, and said, "Geof-frey Dagenham is not here."

"I said nothing about Geoffrey Dagenham, Miss," he blurted out.

I remember as well as possible looking at him and saying—"Didn't you ask about Geoffrey Dagenham?"

"No, I didn't. I never mentioned Geoffrey Dagenham. I asked you where Madge was."

"I am sure I beg your pardon, James," said I; "I mistook you. Madge has gone down to the dressmaker's."

"Do you know when she will be back?" he asked abruptly, taking no notice of my reply.

"No, I don't know when she will be back, but I should fancy she will be rather a long time. I am sure she did not expect you to-day."

"Oh, well, never mind. You can tell her I came." And without another word, or any further salutation or pretence at taking leave, he turned on his heel and re-traced his steps towards the town.

I told Madge when she came back of how James had been, and what he had said and what I had said.

"But Nancy, you little witch," she said, in rather a wondering tone, "what made you say anything about Geoffrey Dagenham?"

"I don't know, Madge," I replied; "it came to me. I am sure he was thinking about Geoffrey Dagenham, and I think he asked me. He said he didn't. I don't know any more than that."

"Oh, well, it doesn't matter a bit," said Madge kindly—she was the kindest of all my brothers and sisters was Madge—"only it was odd you should have happened to hit upon that."

"To hit upon what?" I asked.

"Oh, well, Nancy dear, I don't think you would understand if I told you, but it happens that poor old James is very jealous of Geoffrey Dagenham, and very probably he *was* thinking about him."

"But you have known Geoffrey Dagenham all your life, Madge," I cried. "You knew him long before you ever heard of James Allistair."

"So I did," said Madge, looking away across the charming old garden with a far-off kind of gaze, "so I did—yes, so I did. However, Nancy dear, it's no use saying anything more about it. Don't tell the others, there's a darling. They do worry one so about one's little affairs."

I promised Madge that I would not, and I faithfully kept the secret—if secret it could be called—and about a week after this, well, really, I don't know quite how it happened, but something went wrong with poor James Allistair, and he did not come any more. I met him once or twice when Eve and I were going to school together—yes, we went to school because Father would not be bothered with a governess, he objected to governesses, and of course as there were seven of us we really had not room for one. Besides, as we all went to school, it left Mother free during some part of the day, and, as Father said, let the house get quiet for an hour or two before we came home again.

I have often wondered about James Allistair, and why he gave up coming to the Warren. I suppose he and Madge quarrelled. I tried to find out, but Madge never would talk about it, and although I did give a hint or two to Eve, who was five years older than me and just fifteen, Eve was as close as wax and would not split at any price—dear, dear, there I go again *split,* that is worse than "beer and skittles." I wonder if I shall ever get off the taint of having had four brothers! As I said Eve and I met him several times on our way to and from school, but James never took the least notice of us, in fact, as Eve said, he was excessively rude, he positively cut us dead, and, after all, if he ***had*** quarrelled with our sister it was no fault of ours, as I think Eve would dearly like to have told him,

After that, Geoffrey Dagenham was everlastingly at the Warren, He never seemed to have anything to do, for he used to turn up as soon as breakfast was comfortably over and play tennis with Madge, or with Tom if Madge was not available—he didn't seem particular—and then towards lunch-time he would lounge up to Mother, who generally sat out in the garden on fine mornings, and say to her in a lazy sort of tone—"Well, I must be getting along, Mrs. Reynard." And Mother always looked up in her sweet, dreamy sort of way and said, "Oh, must you? Hadn't you better stay to lunch?" and Geoffrey generally said—"Well, if it wouldn't put you out," to which Mother always answered, "Oh, my dear boy, one more or less makes no difference to me. If you have got nothing better to do, pray stay." He always ***did*** stay, and generally Madge used to come down after changing her dress and say, with an air of great surprise—"What, are you staying ***again,*** Geoffrey? Well, really, I think you had better go back and fetch your box!"

Then in the afternoon, Mother generally went out with Father, You see, she had always been accustomed to spending her mornings without Father, because, of course, when he was in the Service, he always had officer's work and parade and other duty of that kind—you may know what the duty of an officer in barracks is, I can't pretend I do, because I was not born until after Father had given up his command of the 21st. But ever since they had been married, Mother had always gone out in the afternoon with Father, and when he left the Service and became an idle man, she somehow made no change in that respect. As soon as lunch was over, the cob and cart would be brought round, and away they went, unless it was actually raining. Sometimes they made calls, and sometimes they did a little shopping, and sometimes they took a little drive further into the country than the Warren lay; but we were always sure of their being away together between three and half-past five o clock.

I think Madge was unlucky. She was very pretty—well, looking at her from my present standpoint of eighteen and a half years old I am bound to say that she was one of the handsomest girls that I have ever seen, but, at the same time, I am quite sure that she was distinctly unlucky. Geoffrey Dagenham had been a sort of day-boarder at our house for three months, and the brilliant summer was beginning to wane into a still more brilliant autumn, when something happened, and Geoffrey did not come quite so much. The fact was Madge went to stay a week with her godmother, and as Geoffrey was not asked—and as, indeed, their engagement had not been formally announced to the family, that was not to be wondered at—he wandered in and out for a week pretty much as he had been used to do, excepting that he talked to Mother or to Tom instead of to Madge. But at the end of the week, Madge did not come back, and another week slipped by, and another and another, and still she remained the guest of her godmother fifty miles away. It seemed, somehow, quite natural and reasonable that she should stay away in that hand-to-mouth fashion. She was always coming home in two or three days' time, but somehow some fresh gaiety was sure to crop up, and a note would arrive on the morning of the day on which she was expected to be once more with us, a note saying "Dearest Mother, I am so sorry to be still a day or two longer from home, but Lady Margaret particularly wants me to stay for a picnic," or a dinner, or a dance, or a concert, as the case might be, "which takes place to-night. I am really getting very home-sick, but Lady Margaret is so insistent that I thought you would prefer that I should stay."

These letters got to be quite a joke in the family. Tom used to look up at breakfast and say "Well, Madge will be home to-day," and Father used to say, "Ah, where's the letter bag?" and Mother used to take the inevitable letter with a queer little smile, and look across at Father and then say—"Poor darling, she is very home-sick, but it is a ball this time," or "it is a picnic this time," as the case might be. And then Geoffrey used to turn up, and look very glum for ten minutes after the ill-news had been communicated to him, but eventually he would finish the day lounging about very much as he had done before. This went on for about six weeks, and then one day Madge suddenly arrived without any letter at all—and, oddly enough, Geoffrey did not come near the Warren that morning. We found out afterwards that though she had not written to Mother, she had written to him, and to put it shortly, Geoffrey came no more to the Warren for many a long day after receiving Madge's communication, whatever it happened to be.

She arrived in time for lunch, looking very much more grown-up than she had ever done before, with a radiant colour and a glad light in her eyes, and the sunniest smile playing about her mouth.

"Where did you get that ring?" asked Tom, with all a brother's bluntness.

She held her left hand out a little, and made the light of a golden autumn sunbeam play upon the diamonds which clasped the third finger. "Isn't it pretty?" she said.

"What have you done with Geoffrey's ring?" Tom continned.

Tom was devoted to Geoffrey Dagenham.

"Oh, well, of course, it was a dear little ring," said Madge, reddening a little under his inquiring gaze. "Pretty idea, 'Mizpah.' "

"What have you done with it?" asked Tom.

"Well, the fact is I have sent it back to Geoffrey."

"What? You have chucked Geoffrey Dagenham?"

"I am afraid I have," said Madge, looking very conscious.

"Madge!" said Mother.

"I will tell you what, young woman," put in my father in his most commandant voice, "you will get yourself into trouble one of these days if you don't lookout!"

"Oh, yes, dear Daddy, I am afraid I shall," said Madge, "and the sooner I get married, dear, the better it will be for all my family. By-the-bye, I wanted to tell you that somebody is coming to see you this afternoon."

"To see me?" said Father, rather grumpily.

"Yes, dear."

"About you and that ring? Oh, dear, Madge I wish you would get married and have done with it. I am tired of seeing young men on your behalf. Blanche, I think you had better see the young man this time."

"He isn't exactly a *young* man," said Madge.

"Well, this old fellow, then," said Father.

"No, he isn't *old*," my sister objected.

"Well, this man—this ring-giver."

"I have never done that kind of thing, Sep," put in Mother, in her mildest tones, "and of course, you *have,* dear. You are getting quite experienced in giving your consent to Madge's engagements. I think it is a pity to break the rule, isn't it?"

"No, madam, I don't," said Father. "Further-more, I am going out this after-noon, my dear. I have positively promised to be at the Broken Cross at four o'clock. I cannot wait in for your young man, Madge, my dear."

"Oh, there is no hurry," said Madge, easily; "if you see him at tea-time, that will do quite well."

So it happened that when Madge's new lover first came to the Warren, neither Father nor Mother was at home to receive him; in fact, scarcely anybody was at home. Eve and I had a half-holiday, and were engaged for the afternoon and for tea; Charlie and Frank were going to play cricket; and Dick and Tom indignantly went off to see how Geoffrey Dagenham was getting on. So Madge remained alone at home, and what time Mr. Devereux came, or what Madge said to him, I really don't know; but when we younger ones came home, they were all at dinner, and we didn't get so much as a peep at him. Of course, the next morning we were off to school before he appeared again, and it was not until tea that afternoon—which we always had with Mother in the large old drawing-room—that Eve and I met him. Somehow, when we went in, although Madge had a very smart frock on, and was looking very important with all the diamonds twinkling on her left hand, it never occurred to me that the tall, dark, forbidding-looking stranger, who was standing by the tea-table, was the supplanter of Geoffrey Dagenham.

"And these are my younger daughters," said Mother. "This is Eve," indicating my sister, "and this," laying a fond hand upon my shoulder, "is little Nancy."

"How do you do?" said Eve. "How do you do?" said I; then looked at Madge and wondered when *he* was coming. We all talked, and then two of the boys came in and we talked still more, and everybody waited upon everybody, and Mother poured out the tea and was very gracious in consulting the exact taste of the visitor, and presently when Jane had come and cleared the tray and the little table away, he caught hold of me and drew me between his knees.

"Well, so your name is Nancy, little woman, is it?" said he.

"Yes," I answered, "my name is Nancy."

"And a very pretty name too," was his comment. "And now tell me, what do you think of my name?"

"I don't know what your name is," I said promptly.

"Really? My name is Oscar."

"Oscar?" said I, "Oscar—Oscar what?"

"Devereux, of course."

"Oh—but you are not Mr. Devereux?"

"Indeed I am."

"But you can't be Mr. Devereux?"

"My dear little woman, I am indeed."

I looked at Madge. Madge smiled. I looked at Mother. Mother also smiled. I looked at Eve. Eve knew something of what was going on in my mind, and she flashed a glance of distinct inquiry at me. He, still holding me close in his strong grasp, began to tease me.

"I am afraid," said he, "my dear little Nancy, that you don't think very much of me?"

"I—I—never said that," I stammered.

"Now, come, what is it? Are you afraid that I shall lock your sister up or be bad to her? Come, I see there is something in your face. Now, tell me, what is it? Don't you think I shall make a very nice husband for Madge?"

I looked at him. "What have you done with your wife?" I asked.

CHAPTER II.
A STRANGE POWER.

Always there is a black spot upon oar sunshine, and it is, even as I have said, the shadow of ourselves. —CARLYLE.

Thoughts from the tongue that slowly part Glance quick as lightning through the heart. —SIR WALTER SCOTT.

IF I should live to be a hundred years old, I shall never forget the consternation which my question created. Everybody seemed to say "Nancy!" at once. They were all in different tones. Father thundered it, Mother gasped it, my two brothers giggled it, and above all the Babel, of voices, I heard Madge's ejaculation of my name ring out like a broken bell. In his surprise Mr. Devereux had loosened his hold of me. Then he caught my wrists again and said, "Child! What do you mean?"

I stared at him. "I don't mean anything; but you have a wife. You are married."

"How do you know? What do you mean? What are you saying?"

"I didn't know I was saying anything."

"What made you say that at all, Nancy?" asked my father, sternly.

I turned and looked at him. "I don't know, Dad. It came to me. But it is true. Mr. Devereux said just now 'How do you know?' "

"Mr. Devereux," said my father, "I must have an explanation of this?"

"I can give you no explanation," said he, letting my wrists go and getting on to his feet. "If you choose to take the freak of a child's imagination as a certainty, there is nothing for me to say."

"But there *is* something for you to say," said my father. "What made this little girl suggest such a thing?"

He shrugged his shoulders and held out his hand with a deprecatory gesture. "How should I know? Ask the child. She is here."

"Have you ever been married?" said my father.

"Never."

"Can you prove that?"

"Yes, I think that will be very easy to prove. Of course, I admit that the child's extraordinary question startled me for a minute, and when one is very much startled it is difficult to weigh one's words. Come, little Nancy," holding out his hand to me with a great show of kindliness, "you and I are going to be great friends. We won't begin by misunderstanding each other. You will tell your father how you came to put that question to me, won't you?"

"I don't know," I replied; "it came to me. I didn't mean to offend any one. I thought you were married."

"My dear child, how could you tell?"

"I don't know. I thought so, that was all. I didn't know that you were Madge's Mr. Devereux. I didn't hear your name."

"I see. Well, we will be quite friends. We will not go making mistakes about each other in the future."

"Oh, no, I am very sorry," I said—and it was true enough.

I felt bewildered amongst them all, for I saw by Father's face that he was not satisfied, and Madge was looking frightened, and Mother had turned very pale, and as for Mr. Devereux—well, he was like a ghost, he was like chalk and he was trembling. And, after all, what had I said? I had only taken him for somebody who had a wife.

He held out his hand to me—"We will always be good friends, little Nancy," he said, holding his head back and smiling at me.

I put my hand into his and then he kissed me—oh, I remember it so well—and then he sat down. in the same chair in which he had been sitting before, and made me come and sit on his knee while he talked to Mother about all sorts of things; and after half an hour or so, he suddenly spoke to me. "Little Nancy," he said, "what are you thinking of?"

I had been sitting very quietly—if the truth be told, very comfortably—encircled by his arm. I was a slight little thing, very weak and fragile, and fully appreciated being petted and made much of, As he spoke, his hand closed over mine.

"Come," said he, "a penny for your thoughts."

"I was thinking," I said, "of a lady."

"Yes. A nice lady?"

"I don't know. She is tall and she wears a black velvet dress. She has a flashing brooch at her throat—it is like half a star—and it glitters like Madge's ring."

I felt him give a great start, but the others were all listening and he did not stop me from going on.

"She is so pretty, with yellow hair and pink cheeks, and she doesn't look quite straight with her eyes—I think one of her eyes is a little darker than the other. She is in such a pretty room, nearly all blue, and she is standing with her hand on the mantel-shelf and her foot on the fender as if she were waiting."

"Nancy, what are you talking about?" Madge broke in impatiently.

Mr. Devereux withdrew his hand and the vision faded away.

"What did you say, Madge?" I asked.

"What were you talking about? What lady are you describing?"

"I don't know. Yes, I was describing a lady. I am sure I don't know. It is very silly of me. You asked me what I was thinking about, didn't you?"

"To be sure I did, and you promptly conjured up the picture of a charming lady, whom I am sure you have seen somewhere."

"No, I have never seen that lady before," I returned instantly.

"Well, I think you had better go away with Eve," said my father at this point. "Take her away, Eve, she fidgets one. What has come to you, Nancy? You never used to do this sort of thing. It is most unpleasant."

You know, perhaps, the way in which young brothers and sisters can be hustled out of the room when their presence becomes irksome to their elders. I never quite knew whether it was Eye or Madge or the boys or my father who hustled me out of the drawing-room that day. Eve was brimful of curiosity.

"I want to know, Nancy, what made you say that. I believe that man is married. He was in a perfect fright—he was yellow with fright. How can Madge look at him? However Could Madge throw off dear Geoffrey for a horrid, yellow—Ugh!—I wouldn't be Madge for something, that I wouldn't! What made you say it, Nancy?"

"I don't know, I tell you. You ask me such silly questions. I only said what was in my mind. It came to me, I don't know why, and Dad was angry, I am sure he was, and Madge was looking furious——"and then I broke down and ended in wail of despair.

We still had the old nurse who had been with my mother for twenty years—ever since Madge was born, in fact—and hearing me sobbing she came in and gathered me into her capacious arms, holding me fast against her comfortable bosom.

"What is the matter, my blessed pet lamb, my sweet angel bird? Tell old Nursie what it is, dearest."

"I don't know, Nurse. But I do feel so worried. People are always asking me silly questions, and then when I answer them they don't like it. They get cross and they go white and do all sorts of things. I don't know. There is a horrid man downstairs that Madge is going to marry. I don't like him, Nurse."

"Eh, my lamb, but that is bad hearing."

"And he asked me what I thought, and I cannot tell lies about it—Father says it is mean and vulgar to tell lies, and Mother looks like a dying duck in a thunderstorm if we suggest such a thing, as if, if we were to tell a lie, she would have a fit on the spot, and then when I tell the truth, it sets everybody by the ears. I only said what I thought."

"And what did you think, my lamb?"

"I don't know, I forget. Don't worry me, Nurse."

"My dear honey, I won't worry you, but you seemed in trouble and I thought I could help you out of it."

That was the beauty of Nurse, she never did worry us. She held me on her knee and rocked me to and fro in the big rocking-chair until I had forgotten all the disagreeable sensations that had happened since our return home that day, and presently we had our usual substantial nursery tea and I went to bed, for once not the least little bit jealous that Eve was going down to dessert and I was not.

Somehow after this—I really don't know how it was—but home seemed rather different, You see, there was always that tall, black, yellow Mr. Devereux about, and somehow I was always glad to get out of the room when he was in. I didn't like him. He always smiled at me when we met and seemed very pleased to see me. He showed his teeth when he smiled—they were very white, and they made me think of the wolf in the story of Red Riding Hood. So, somehow, all the old comfortable, chummy sort of feeling disappeared. You could not go down to the shrubbery but you had a chance of coming across Madge and Mr. Devereux sitting sentimentally on one of the rustic seats, and if you avoided the shrubbery and went towards the south garden, where the peaches grew—although, of course, the peaches were all over long since—you were pretty sure to come across them in the old summer-house; and as it got colder and we were not able to be so much out of doors, it seemed to make no difference which room you chose to go into—they were always there!

Really, life got to be quite a burden to us. Father and Mother went out earlier and stayed longer, Tom and Dick seemed to have quite exchanged positions with poor dear Geoffrey Dagenham, and Charlie and Frank had never been so much in the old nursery for years. Now it was better for Eve than it was for me. You see, she was fifteen, creeping up to sixteen, and I was only just turned ten. If Charlie and Frank cheeked her, she could just bang them; but if Charlie and Frank cheeked me, I hadn't a chance. So it was not always comfortable for me in the old nursery even when Nurse herself was there. And Charlie and Frank expected me to do all the fagging for them and get- none of the fun. *I* had to go down and coax cook to give me raisins, and I got none but what I helped myself to on the way up-stairs; *I* had to go down and ask Mother for an extra sixpence to buy something they wanted, but they always said after I had got it that girls were duffers and could not expect to play with boys. I really was tired of being shut out of Mother's drawing-room and kept up in that nursery, given over, as it were, to the boys. Of course, I might have told, and I might have got the boys into trouble, because Father was always down upon anything like bullying us girls or anything of the kind; but what would have been the good of that? They would have called me sneak, and tell - pie, and tittle-tattle, and *Miss* Nancy for years afterwards, and life would have been a perfect purgatory; it was bad enough as it was. So I never sneaked. I made up my mind to bear it, but I can tell you I didn't like Madge's Mr. Devereux—that I didn't—for he was the cause of everything.

What a difference that man's coming had made to the dear old Warren! There was a sense of unrest over everything, and I think Madge felt it most of anybody. Almost every day he brought her some fresh gift, until really she had so many rings at last that she could not possibly wear them all at once; and instead of being elated, as most girls would have been, she seemed weighed down by them, and she got to look pinched and ill and mopey. I don't know what was the matter with her, because she said over and over again that she was enormously fond of Mr. Devereux. I didn't like him and Nurse didn't like him, but Father said he was very satisfactory, and Mother said he was devoted, and Charlie and Frank said he was a brick, but I think that was because he had more than once tipped them a sovereign each.

I remember the last thing before Tom went off to Sandhurst I heard him talking to Mother about things and he told Mother that Oscar Devereux was a beast. I remember it quite well, because I was sitting in the little rocking-chair in the big bow-window of the drawing-room, just behind the muslin curtains, trying to read "The Little Tin Soldier" by the grey afternoon light. Mother was sitting by the fire and Tom was leaning his back against the chimney-shelf, and I heard him say distinctly—"It is no use your saying anything else, Mother, the man is a beast!"

"My dear Tom," said Mother, "I hope not, because Madge seems very fond of him. She says she is very much in love with him, and I am sure I hope there is no reason for your dislike of him."

"I can't give you a reason, Mother," said Tom, "but I have an instinct against him."

"Don't you think, dear, that you are rather prejudiced with being such a friend of poor Geoffrey's?" said Mother, mildly. "Of course, I myself would much rather have had Geoffrey for my son-in-law of the two; but we must not forget, in our liking for Geoffrey, that it is Madge to whom the great difference will be made."

"Madge always pretended she was so fond of Geoffrey," growled Tom.

"Well, she did, dear; but these things are so often taken out of our hands by circumstances or by change of mood. You see, she has known Geoffrey all her life, and really, I don't know, Tom, I wish it could be decided for us by somebody who could really look into the future a little. Sometimes I think she is not happy and sometimes she seems deliriously so, and then I get thinking of poor Geoffrey, and really I can't sleep at night for it."

"Why did the Governor give his consent; that's what I want to know? What is this Jack-a-Dandy? Where did he come from?" said Tom, thrusting his hands deep down into his trousers pockets.

"Well, dear, he gave the most excellent references. He referred your father to his lawyers and his bankers and to his oldest friends, and of course, he is making handsome settlements, we can't forget that, and with all you boys, Madge can't expect much. Indeed, I must do Mr. Devereux the justice to say that he waived all idea of looking for a penny with her, and of course he is very good looking."

"Good looking!" grunted Tom. "Yes, just about as good looking as a Berkshire pig!"

"Oh, no, my dear Tom! Be honest, be just, The man is very good looking and a very fine man and he has charming manners, and of course he is generosity itself towards Madge."

"Generosity!" growled Tom. "Well, I don't know. He has made her look like one of those big advertisement sheets of brooches and bangles and rings and things. I don't like to see Madge covered all over with diamonds, as if she had suddenly turned pawnbroker or something of that kind."

"Well, dear, well," said Mother soothingly, "we must leave it to Madge to decide. She is not like a very young girl, as if it were Eve, for instance. She is twenty. You know, dear boy, I had married and was thinking about your teething when I was Madge's age."

"Yes, I suppose so," said he unwillingly. "But I am very fond of Madge and I don't like the fellow."

"Well, try, dear, try to like him," said Mother in her mild and soothing voice.

But Tom went off to Sandhurst without accomplishing that part of Mother's behests, and for a little time life went on pretty much the same. Mr. Devereux stayed mostly at one of the hotels in Minchester and day-boarded with us, and Madge got thinner and the Warren got more uncomfortable, and the wedding day was fixed. And then something happened. It was me, of course—everything that happened at the Warren might have been summed up in that one little personal pronoun—and it came about in this way.

They were all out one day and I was very busy reading "Little Women"—which is rather soft, don't you think? but still, interesting—by the light of the drawing-room fire. We had a great big white bear skin lying in front of the fire which, with a cushion, made a most delightful place for reading before the lamps were lighted, and whilst I was still there, they all came in together—Mother and the Colonel, and Madge and Mr. Devereux, I believe that they had been out together, and as Mother went to ring the bell for tea she very nearly walked on to me.

"My dear child!" she said. "I almost stepped upon you! Why don't you have a lamp? It is most bad for your eyes to be reading by the firelight."

I was not accustomed to get up, looking as if I were going to be killed the next minute, when Mother said anything like that, so I didn't move—I was very comfortable where I was—but Mr. Devereux sat down in the big chair and lifted me clean off the rug on to his knee.

"Why, my dear little woman," said he in his most gracious tones, "supposing you had fallen asleep and a big cinder had hopped out of the fire on to you and frizzled you all up, what then?"

I don't know whether I wriggled, but, anyhow, he took hold of my wrist pretty firmly with his left hand, that arm being passed round me. I daresay such a question might have been very amusing for a *little* girl, which I was not, and somehow I never thought of answering him; but I really don't know what prompted me to say what I did, for while he was still grasping my wrist, I looked up at him—"Why did you strike that lady?" I asked. "Did she hurt her head when she fell?"

CHAPTER III.
113, GREAT PAKENHAM STREET.

Circumstances are like clouds, continually gathering and bursting; while we are laughing, the seed of trouble is put into the wide arable land of events. —KEATS.

Conviction comes like lightning; In vain you seek it, and in vain you fly. —CRABBE.

WHEN I asked Mr. Devereux that question—"Why did you strike that lady? Did she hurt her head when she fell?" he behaved in the most extraordinary manner I have ever seen anyone behave in my life. First of all, he upset me—yes, really, for he jumped up from his chair so suddenly and with such a horrid, ugly word on his lips, that I found myself sprawling on the big bear-skin rug before I knew where I was.

"Mr. Devereux!" said Mother in an astonished tone.

"My dear Mrs. Reynard," said he apologetically, "I must ask you to forgive me, but the truth is your little daughter here really almost startled me out of my senses. My good child," he went on, taking hold of my wrist and helping me up from the rug, "why do you always ask these strange, mysterious questions of me? Who is the lady that seems to be mixed up with me in your mind?"

I could feel and see that he was trembling violently, but he held out his hand with a great show of friendliness.

"I don't know," I replied. "I—I—only said what came to me."

"But what made you speak of a lady at all?" he asked as his fingers closed over mine.

"Because I saw her," I replied. "You *did* strike her, didn't you?"

"I strike a lady—strike a woman! Really, child there is something quite uncanny about you. What have you in your mind? Don't you like me?"

"Yes, I like you when you are sitting here with Mother and Madge and all of us, but I don't like you when I see that lady."

"But what lady?"

"Oh, she is very tall and fair, and there is something different about her eyes. She fell with her head on the fender."

"My God!" he muttered under his breath.

For once my mother roused herself out of her charming simplicity.

"Nancy, come here" she said. "Now tell me, who told you anything about this lady or about Mr. Devereux?"

"Nobody, Mother," I replied.

"What made you say that?"

"I don't know. It came to me."

"How did it come to you?"

I looked from her to him and back, then to Madge and back to Mother again— "I cannot tell you—I—I didn't mean to say anything to vex any of you. I am very sorry."

"You have not said anything to vex us, dear, but it is so strange. We want to know—I am sure Mr. Devereux must want to know quite as much as I do—what made you say anything about this lady at all."

"I don't know," I answered; and it was true, my mind was a perfect blank.

"Where did you see this lady?" Mother persisted.

"Where did I see her? I don't know."

I was frightened by their grave looks, and, childlike, I began to cry. My mother got up at once and took me out of the room.

"You must take no notice. She is only a child," I heard her say to Mr. Devereux. "Children do take such strange unaccountable fancies," she added as we reached the door.

"Mother," said I, when the door had safely closed behind us, "I didn't take a fancy."

"No, dear, but something must have made you say that. You see you have several times almost startled Mr. Devereux out of his senses. What *did* make you say it, dear?"

"I don't know, Mother," I said anxiously. "I didn't mean to say anything, but sometimes I speak as if it were not me at all. I can't help it."

"But how came you to see Mr. Devereux strike a lady, dear?"

I suddenly sprang away from my mother. "He *did* strike her, he *did* strike her, Mother, and she fell with her head on the fender, and she has eyes of a different colour."

"But how could you see it, my dear? He has been near nobody. It is ridiculous. There has been nobody here of the description that you gave. How could you see what was not there to see?"

"But he *did* strike her," I said.

"What did she do when she fell?"

"She struck her head against the fender."

"Well, and what did she do then?"

"I don't know."

"Did you see it?"

"I think so. I am not sure. I don't remember."

My mother laid her hand upon my shoulder and gave me a little shake—oh, no, I don't mean to express an unkind shake, for Mother was never unkind to anyone in her life, but just to recall me to my senses, as if I was saying something, I didn't know what.

"My dear Nancy, pull yourself together," she said, speaking quite firmly, "what do you mean? My dear Nancy, you *must* remember whether you saw it or whether you didn't see it. You know that even little girls have no right to say that they saw things unless they are quite sure, and I, your mother, tell you that there has been no such lady here?"

"I don't know," I said, breaking down into tears again, "I do feel so worried; you all worry me. I only say what is in my head here, but you worry me as if I were doing it on purpose. I cannot help speaking when I feel like that."

"But how do you feel?"

"I don't know."

"Did you see this lady?"

"Yes, I think I did."

"Or do you think you were dreaming for a moment?" said Mother.

I caught at the suggestion as a drowning man would catch at a straw—"Yes, I think perhaps I was dreaming—I don't know."

"Do you ever feel like that with any one else?" Mother asked.

"No, I don't think so. I don't mean to feel like that with him. I—I—can't say anything more, Mother, because I don't know."

"There, there, then we won't say anything more about it," said my mother very kindly. "You shall go up and have tea with Nurse. Don't come down to-night, dear, you are excited and upset. By and by when Madge is gone, when she is married, you will feel differently about this."

I did have tea with Nurse that day, and I remember she gave me some honey, and then Jane came up and said that the Colonel wanted me to go down to the drawing-room again. I went down as soon as Nurse had made me tidy and had put me on a very smart clean pinafore.

"Why, young woman,' said the Colonel in his loudest voice, when I appeared in the drawing-room, "What do you mean by deserting us in this way? I cannot do without you."

"I have been having tea with Nurse," I answered.

"Oh, have you? Then I hope you enjoyed it, but I didn't enjoy my tea without you. Come and sit here, my Nancy."

He was sitting up in the corner of a very big lounge and he patted the seat beside him as an invitation that I should share it. I was very fond of my father. He was so big and jovial and so unbothering. Somehow, even when he was vexed about things, he didn't worry me. I think, you know, with children it is often so, some people worry them and some people don't. Now Mr. Devereux always worried me from first to last. I found afterwards that Father knew nothing of what I had said to him that afternoon, and so he made me get out the little table and the box of dominoes and went on teaching me that delightful game quite unconscious that I and Mr. Devereux had contrived less than an hour ago to thoroughly upset each other.

The dressmaker came up presently to fit Madge for several dresses. Jane came in and fetched her and she gave a laughing apology to Mr. Devereux and to all of us for having to go.

"Mother," she said, "I do wish you would come and run your eagle eye over them, because, you know, Miss Shepperton is very slippery sometimes, and pretends that one's back is perfect when it is simply a mass of wrinkles."

So Mother, laughing too, got up and went away with her. This reduced the company in the drawing-room to the Colonel, Mr. Devereux and me.

"Do you know this game, Devereux?" said my father.

The Colonel was a very polite man, He never left anybody to feel out in the cold and it was a sort of instinct with him to at once include Mr. Devereux in our game.

"Well, I have played it abroad sometimes. It is a great game in Gemany, you know."

"Yes, I know it is," said the Colonel, "it is a very good game, a very fine game, and little Nancy here has the making of a player in her."

I had left my place on the great couch and was sitting in an arm-chair opposite to my father. Mr. Devereux came and leant upon the back of it and pointed now and again with his little finger to the piece which he thought I ought to play. I wished with all my heart that he would go away. I was not comfortable with him there, after what had taken place. I felt, somehow, as if I preferred him to be on the other side of the room and not leaning quite close to me. Besides, I was playing against Father and did not want to be helped and advised by anybody else, even if he did happen to know the game better than I did. That was never my idea of equal rights in playing anything. I daresay that I fidgetted a little, and that perhaps somewhat distracted the Colonel's attention, for instead of keeping it closely fixed upon the game, as was his regular habit, he kept up a running conversation with Mr. Devereux. They discussed various places on the Continent, both German and French, and then my father said that all laid and done he preferred England to any other place in the world.

"I have been everywhere," he remarked, "and lived everywhere and seen everything and tried everything, and I have come to the conclusion that a good country town in England is the best place in the world, both to live in and bring your children up in."

"You prefer it to London?" said Mr. Devereux.

"Very much," said my father. "I like London for a week at a time, but somehow I get kind of home-sick if I ever stop longer. You see, I have never been used to it, I have never even spent a long leave there—not entirely, that is to say. A week at a time is about my form."

"Yes? Then, of course, you never know but the outside of Town. You don't know it socially in any way if you spend but a short time there at once."

"That is true," said my father, "but I don't know that I want to know it socially. Now down here, in this quiet place, I get as good a time socially as I could get anywhere. There are plenty of very nice people in and about Minchester, and you know there is always this, Devereux, that here one is somebody, and in London one is only one of a few millions."

"Yes, there is a good deal in that, I admit, though I could not live out of London myself for long. I have not been out of London, since I left Eton, for as long a time together as I have been away from it now."

"And you live in the Albany?" said my father, holding a finger and thumb upon a row of dominoes in front of him the better to select one.

"113, Great Pakenham Street," I remarked.

I don't know what made me say it; I have never known what made me say it except it was instinct.

My father looked up and said, "Hullo, Pussy!" and Mr. Devereux bounced off the arm of my chair on which he had been sitting, crying in a passionate voice, "By Heaven, but there is something in this! What do you know about Great Pakenham Street?"

I came to myself with a sort of shudder. "Oh, Daddy," putting my hand out for protection to my father, "I am so frightened!"

"My dear child," said the Colonel, "what *is* the matter? What made you say anything about Great Pakenham Street?"

"I don't know. I don't know. It came to me. I could not help it. I don't know what Great Pakenham Street is," and then I looked round at him. "What is Great Pakenham Street, Mr. Devereux?" I asked. "Where is it? What made me say that?"

"Heaven knows," he replied furiously; "but, Colonel Reynard, I can't stand much more of this! I never come near this child but she has got some mysterious communication to make about me. I—ah—h! But of one thing I am convinced. All. this is a plant; she has been put up to it."

"Sir!" cried my father.

"I can't help it. I daresay you will be offended but I can't help it. First of. all she tells me I am married; then she describes some woman that none of you have ever heard of; then this very afternoon she asked me why I struck her and if she hurt her head falling against the fender! What does she mean by it? Now you ask me if

I live in the Albany, and she gives an address of some rooms where I—did—live—once."

The words seemed to come out one by one like a man speaking against his will.

"My father turned round to me. "Nancy," he said, "I have never found you out in a lie in my life. You will tell me the truth, child?"

"Why, of course, Dad," I replied.

"Who told you anything about Great Pakenham Street?"

"Nobody. I give you my word, Dad. I don't know what Great Pakenham Street is. It came—I cannot help these things—they *come* to me! It is Mr. Devereux here, when he comes close to me things come into my head. I am only a little girl. I don't know what they mean. Something made me say it. I never saw any Great Pakenham Street in my life. I don't know where it is. I am frightened, Father."

"And by the Heaven above," said my father, "it is enough to make you frightened! Devereux, I must speak plainly and seriously to you about this. There is something underhand, there is something behind all this, there is something in your life which has not been explained to us, and I am not going to let my young daughter do anything for which she may have cause to repent—for which we may all be bitterly sorry by and by. This child is a child—a mere baby. I never, as I said just now, found her out in an untruth in my life—I don't believe, by Jove, that a child of mine would know how to tell one—but it seems to me," standing up and eyeing Oscar Devereux very keenly, "that some power of which we know nothing may have put these suggestions into this child's mind for the purpose of warning us, who cannot see so far as some unexplained power above us or around us. Mr. Devereux, you must forgive what I am going to say, but I must ask you to consider from to-day that there is a hiatus in your engagement to my daughter. You must give me a few days, and stay away from the Warren, in order that I may seek out this address which has come to this child like a thing of magic, that I may satisfy myself and my wife that there is no real reason for this extraordinary information coming to her. I know that you may think it very hard, but I consider that I have no choice in the matter."

I, child-like, was staring at Mr. Devereux with all my eyes. He turned white, grey, almost blue while my father was speaking. Something in his throat seemed to choke him and he put up his hand as if to help himself to breathe, then he bit his lip and turned and looked at me—such a look! Child as I was, it filled me, not with fear, but it seemed to shrivel me all up; but I did not turn my eyes from his, I stared at him straight with all my strained attention fixed upon him. He only looked at me for a moment, then he turned away with a shudder and put his hand up so as to shield his eyes.

"That child has got the evil eye," said he. "Colonel Reynard, I give up my engagement from this moment. My marriage with Madge can never be. Don't trouble to enquire into my past, make my peace with Madge"—and there his voice broke and a suspicious quiver passed across his lips—"I love her, Colonel Reynard. You will perhaps never know how much, but all the love in the world would not compensate for being continually in touch with this little conscience here," and then he just glanced at me and turned away sharp, as if I had been a looking-glass and he could see his guilty soul in it.

"Am I to understand, Devereux," said my father, speaking very gravely and in his most commanding voice, "that you give up your engagement entirely without enquiry, without question?"

"Yes."

"Then I am to understand that there *is* something in what this child says?"

"Oh, understand what you like."

"But," said my father, "do you expect me not to make any enquiry?"

"Colonel Reynard," said the other, "I expect nothing. I implore you to let me pass out of your life, as if I had never come into it."

CHAPTER IV.
FREE OF THE SPELL.

Look not mournfully into the past; it comes not back again, Wisely improve the present; it is thine. —*Footprints of Angels.*

How slow, how sure, how swift, The sands within each glass, The brief illusive moments pass! Half unawares we mark their drift Till the awakened heart cries out—Alas! Alas, the fair occasion fled, The precious chance to action all unwed! And murmurs in its depths the old refrain— Had we but known betimes what now we know in vain! —STEDMAN.

BEFORE we could recover from our astonishment, and indeed, from our dismay, Mr. Devereux had flung himself out of the room. We heard the shutting of the hall-door a moment later, and knew that he had gone. My father sat down again on the wide lounge and looked at me in consternation and dismay—"Nancy, my little woman," he said "you have done it!"

"But what have I done?" I asked.

"I am afraid you have sent that fellow about his business. What put it into your mind to say those things?"

I began to whimper a little as children will do. "I don't know, Daddy, they come. I can't help it. Something came when he said to you—the Alderney—what did he say?"

"The Albany," said my father, "the Albany."

"Something inside me said '113 Great Pakenham Street,' I don't know what. Do you think he ever did live there?"

"He said he did. Now the question is," my father went on, "how are we going to break this to Madge. I believe Madge was very fond of the fellow. I don't believe he will ever come back again."

But Madge did. She came down presently, wearing a pretty evening frock, a black gauzy affair with big transparent sleeves, and her only ornament was her own pretty name made in diamonds. This she wore at one side of the square cut bodice.

"Well?" she said, then looked round. "Why, where is Oscar?"

My father got up, "Madge, my dear child," he answered, "I am afraid that I have got something very unpleasant to tell you about Oscar."

"About Oscar?"

"About Devereux. He was watching me playing dominoes with the child, in fact, he was sitting on the edge of her chair, and he and I were talking quite idly as we played. We were talking about the difference of living in foreign towns and in English towns, between provincial towns and London. I told him I could not live in London and he said he could not live out of it. I said, goodness knows idly enough, 'You live in the Albany?' and before he could answer, Nancy here said in a dreamy sort of tone—'113 Great Pakenhim Street!' My dear girl, the effect upon Devereux was magical. He looked like a—well, really, I don't want to hurt your feelings, but he looked like a convicted felon. I told him flatly that I would have to consider the engagement temporarily over, that I might enquire into his past life, and he promptly chucked up the whole thing."

"Was he offended?" said Madge.

She had grown very pale and her hand was trembling very much. She didn't seem angry or even particularly surprised.

"No, but he could not look at the child, and he says she has the evil eye—Such bosh! Such rubbish!" my father went on contemptuously. "And yet, as I told him, I feel convinced that the man has a past into which we cannot enquire. I *shall* enquire into it."

Madge put out her hand and laid it upon the Colonel's arm. "Dear Daddy," she said, "don't do anything of the kind. I won't say that I have been expecting this, yet, at the same time, I have been in a measure prepared for it. At all events, do nothing until some of us have heard from him. We shall do that surely. Little Nancy, what made you say it?"

"I don't know," I replied, "I didn't mean to say it."

"You will write down the address?" she went on, turning to my father.

"Yes, I shall do so. I will do it now."

He went as far as the door, then turned back and put his arm round Madge, "My dearest," he said, in a very gentle voice, "I am afraid all this has hurt you terribly."

"I don't know," said Madge restlessly, "I—I—have felt somehow lately as if I were in prison, as if I were in a bottle with the cork put in tight. It hasn't seemed to be me of late. He has been everything that is good and kind and considerate to me, still, I have never seemed to be quite a free agent. I jilted poor Geoffrey Dagenham for his sake and I don't think that I was as kind to him as I ought to have been. Something made' me do things that I should not have done a year ago. I don't know, I don't know, dear Daddy, what has come to me. I wish you would promise me something."

"Yes, of course, I will promise you anything."

"Don't talk to me about this just for a little. We shall be having a letter, we **must** be having a letter; I have all his rings and diamonds and ornaments and all sorts of things that I could not keep if he is really gone away. I want to go upstairs and think it out quietly. You can tell Mother I will talk about it to-morrow."

Well, in ten minutes or so Mother came down again, all unknowing of what had happened.

"Why, where is Oscar?" she asked, looking round the well-lighted room.

"My dear," said Father, pulling her down on the lounge beside him, "something has happened."

"Something has happened? What?"

"Well, I am afraid Devereux is gone, or rather I know that he is gone."

"Gone? Where?" asked my mother.

"Gone for good."

And then he related to her everything that had happened, and she in her turn told him of what I had said when they had come in that afternoon.

"And you think he has gone?" said my mother. "Do you think there is anything in it?"

"My dear, if you had seen the fellow's face, you would have thought there was everything in it, and where this little maid gets the clue to everything, as she does, simply passes my comprehension."

Well, they talked and they talked; but all the talk in the world doesn't lessen a mystery where no outside information comes to help, Mr. Devereux did not come back. Madge remained up in her bedroom. Nurse came and fetched me away to bed, and as I kissed Mother and said good-night to her, she whispered to me to say nothing of what had happened, to keep my own counsel, lest I turned my innocent words into mischief. I promised her and with that she was satisfied, for although we seven were not in any sense perfect, any one of us would have scorned to break a promise once given.

I think from what I heard Mother say the next morning, that she had expected Mr. Devereux would send a letter by hand to explain his abrupt departure to Madge, but no letter came that night, at least, so I gathered when I entered the dining-room in the morning and found Father turning over his letters.

"Not a letter from that fellow again," I heard him say.

"I quite thought that there would have been one by hand last night," said Mother. "Is there nothing? Are you sure?"

"Perfectly certain. There is not a letter for Madge at all. Surely, he would never go away, turn tail, bolt like this without making some enplanation to the girl who was so nearly married to him. Besides he told me last night that he loved her——"

"Hush!" said Mother, "she is coming."

Madge came in accompanied by Eve. She was looking pale, but not at all as if she had been crying or anything of that kind. She was wearing a pretty crimson dress of some soft woollen material, she had a little brooch at her throat that Geoffrey Dagenham had given her years and years before, and she was not wearing a ring of any kind whatever. She said good-morning to Mother in quite a cheerful tone and she went round and laid her head for a minute against the Colonel's cheek and never so much as asked whether there was a letter for her. I thought it very queer, and I am sure, from the looks that Mother cast at Father, that they both thought it very queer too. Tom, of course, had been gone to Sandhurst ever so long, but Dick was at home, and he, not knowing anything of the fuss that had taken place the previous night, asked her almost before she had seated herself where all her grand rings were.

Madge held out her two pretty hands in front of her. "I am bit off rings, Dick," she said looking at him quite gaily. "I shall take fetters, my dear boy, quite soon enough without fettering myself now. I don't think I shall ever wear a ring again."

"H'm! I suppose you will when you're married."

"But I am not married yet," said Madge.

"Oh, that is the way the cat jumps, is it?"

"Something like that," said she—then helped herself to a piece of bread and butter and stirred her coffee reflectively.

Later in the day the anxiously looked-for letter came. It came by the second post and Jane brought it in to Madge in quite an ordinary way upon a salver.

"Oh, for me?" said Madge. "Thank you, Jane."

She opened it, read it once, twice, a third time.

"Mother," she said at last, turning and looking at Mother, who was stitching away quite industriously at a bit of fancy work, "you would like to see this, wouldn't you?"

"If it pleases you to show me, darling," said Mother gently.

"Yes, I would rather that you would see it, but I don't think you need tell any one else about it. Perhaps as it mentions Nancy, she might see it too. I am going out."

Mother caught her hand before she looked at the letter. "Darling, are you sure that you axe not feeling this very deeply?"

Madge looked down. "No, Mother. I begin to think that I have not been myself for a long time. I begin to think that there are many things in life which are quite uncanny and which people ridicule because they do not want to believe them; but I feel quite sure now that I had no free choice in my engagement. I had not known for months past what it was to have a will of my own. I seem to have been always guided by some subtle and invisible power, as subtle and invisible as that power which prompted Nancy to say things of which she absolutely knew nothing, things which disclosed the truth. I feel better able to breathe this morning than I have done for a long time," and then she just gently patted Mother's hand and went away leaving us alone together.

Mother read the letter. "Nancy," she said to me, when she had read it to the very end, "I don't know whether I ought to show you this letter or not. You are only a little girl, and yet you have become mixed up in your sister's affairs in a very unusual and strange manner. If I show it to you I can trust you to keep it to yourself?"

"Oh, yes, Mother," I answered.

"I don't know what strange power enabled you to say what you did, but this is what Mr. Devereux says to Madge."

She handed me the letter, which was written in a hand so fine, so clear, so round, that I was easily able to read it.

"My own Madge," it said, "I am writing this letter to wish you good-bye for always. Your father will have told you what happened last night while you were gone up-stairs. Well, it was not very much, but it amounts to this much—that I cannot carry out my engagement with you. Not that I do not love you, Madge, I think you know that, but I cannot marry the sister of your little Nancy. I don't know what there is about that child which is so antagonistic to me, she has always seemed pleasant and nice with me, but every now and again she comes out with these fearful assertions, and they all point to something that is true. I am not, a saint, I have never pretended to you that I am a saint. There are chapters in the life of every man which he would not have read to the whole world in a clear and ringing voice. There are leaves turned down in my past which I would not turn back myself, which I would not have my wife read for the riches of the universe. It is all very simple. The child has the gift of second sight, and she sees through me from time to time as easily as she could look through a pane of glass into another room. I have not been worse than most other men, but I cannot stand living under a microscope, I cannot face having my very thoughts laid bare from time to time by that terrible child. So it is better that we should part. I don't feel somehow that I need say much to you about your love. In all our intercourse, Madge, the love has been mine, the persuasion has been mine, the influence has been mine. I think that you have only submitted. Your feeling has not been a more active one than that. I would have loved you, yes, I would have loved you with all my heart and for all my life, but now that strange and inexplicable mystery has come in between us and I can only bid you farewell, my dear love, a farewell for all time. Do me a last favour. I have given you some trifles as pledges of my affection. Will you keep them? Will you wear them sometimes in memory of a man who had lived through a very stormy life, and who had for a little while hoped to glide into the peaceful haven of your true affection? It is the last favour that I ask of you and feeling that you will grant it makes me very happy.

"YOURS, OSCAR."

"Now, Nancy," said my mother, when I had read it to the end, "what he says about the second sight is nonsense."

"But what *is* the second sight?" I asked.

"Oh, my dear child, it is the power of being able to see things that are not on the surface, being able to look into the soul of another human being as clearly as you can look at other objects with your eyes. I don't believe in it. I think that he must himself unconsciously have given you the clue to some story in the past which he would not like your father, or myself, or Madge to know anything about. You know, dear, that when we have done Wrong, we are always afraid of that wrong coming to light. Shakespeare says, 'Conscience makes cowards of us all'; and I am sadly afraid that conscience may have made a coward of Oscar Devereux."

I was still holding the letter in my hand, and just then, somehow, my mother's voice seemed to fade away into the distance, the room to be blotted out, and myself transported into a room, large, dull, and filled with very heavy furniture. Oscar Devereux sat at the table writing a letter. He finished the letter, put it into the envelope, addressed it, took a stamp from a small box at hand, and fixed it to the envelope. Then he opened a drawer and took out a pistol. . . . "Oh! Don't—Don't shoot!" I cried.

CHAPTER V.
'TIS WISER TO FORGET.

Life is longer, greater, purer, nobler, beyond comparison, for all the secret ties and loving words of home. —GARBETT.

There's a Divinity that shapes our ends, Rough hew them how we will.
—*Hamlet.*

FOR the first time in my life I fainted. I don't myself know or recollect anything about the actual occurrence. I remember seeing in a dim sort of way, Oscar Devereux sitting at a table writing, and then seeing him pull out a pistol from a drawer and put it to his head. I screamed out, and the next thing I knew was that I was lying on the floor with my head upon my Mother's lap, and Nurse and Father were standing near us.

"It is all right. She is coming to," I heard Mother say, and then they lifted me up a little and held some water to my lips. Well, as a matter of fact, there was brandy in it.

"I don't like it," I said, when I had tasted it.

"My dear, take a little sip of it," said Nurse, "you are not very well and it is only a tiny taste of brandy. It won't hurt you and will do you more good than anything else."

I took it, of course. We were always accustomed to do what Nurse told us, because she was the kind of woman who never asked us to take anything, except with a very good reason, and for years past we had been in the habit of always pleasing her in such matters if we could do so.

"Why am I down here?" I asked, presently.

"Oh, my dear, you are a little faint," said Mother, "but you are better now, aren't you?" looking down at me anxiously.

"Oh, yes, I am all right, I think. I don't think there is anything the matter with me."

"I think, Ma'am," said Nurse, "that I will take the dear lamb up stairs and keep her quiet on the nursery sofa for a while."

"And I think," said Father, "that I will just run down and fetch Somers. I don't like this sort of thing happening, and it is better to hear what he says about it."

"Oh, I am not ill, Father," I declared. "I really don't think there is anything the matter with me."

"Well, my dear, I will just let Somers have a look at you."

I was a little fragile thing and Nurse picked me up in her arms, and carried me off to the nursery which was on the first floor, as easily as if I had been a baby. Then she put me down on the wide old couch, which she drew near to the fire, and with a couple of pillows under my head and an eiderdown flung over my feet, I was as comfortable as I had ever been in my life.

Dr. Somers came presently and evidently had heard all that there was to tell before he was brought up into the nursery. He examined me very closely, asked me a great many questions, and told Mother that I was to be kept very quiet indeed, that I was suffering more or less from shock. I didn't know then what shock meant, but I suppose now that it was the horror of the vision in which I had seen Oscar

Devereux raise his hand against his own life.

It was years before I knew the actual end of that sad and tragic story. I must have been quite fifteen before I discovered that when in my excitement I let his letter fall from my hand, it cut off the vision and so mercifully prevented me from seeing the end of that awful tragedy. Even then, I was not told this in so many words, for from the day that I fainted in my mother's drawing-room at the Warren, until I was more than fifteen, I was more frail and weakly than even I had been before. It was quite by accident that I discovered then that Oscar Devereux actually died by his own hand at his chambers in the Albany. What was the actual story of his life and what my father discovered in his subsequent enquiries, I have never found out yet, but, you see, my father and mother now, as then, are more than anxious to prevent my thoughts reverting to that time, or to anything which will remind me that I am gifted with the power which, in many cases, is the inheritance of the seventh child.

That autumn, I continued to be very frail and weak, and Dr. Somers advised my parents that I should be taken to the south of France or somewhere on the Riviera, and kept during the winter as quietly and with as little excitement as was possible. Now, you must remember that there were seven of us. True, I was the youngest, but Frank, who was next to me, was only a year and a month or two my senior, and Charlie was but thirteen at this time, and very serious were the discussions which took place between my father and mother, in their anxiety that I should be best cared for, in a way which would not too much interfere with the interest of my brothers and sisters.

Eventually, I started with Mother and Nurse for a little town on the Italian coast, a little town lying between Genoa and Leghorn, where the sun always seemed to shine, where the skies always seemed to be radiant, and the blue waters of the Mediterranean but reflected the brighter glory of the skies above. It had been suggested that Madge should go with us, but Madge herself stoutly declined the expedition.

"No, dear Mother," she replied, when the question was mooted to her, "you are taking Nurse with you, and it is quite out of the question for me to go also. While I am here, you will have your mind at rest, and as I ail nothing there is no earthly reason why I should go. I will look after the Colonel and after all the others for you and let you know very often how we are getting on. So you can go off with a free conscience, and take care of Nancy as comfortably as if we were all with you, instead of being left behind."

That winter by the sunny shores of the Mediterranean did wonders for me. There were several other English families there, some with children, some without, and we were all very friendly and had quite a splendid time together, and as everything went well at home Mother was perfectly happy and contented in her mind. Of course, we heard from them all pretty often. The Colonel, indeed, wrote twice a week regularly, and Madge almost as often; while the boys' letters were decidedly intermittent, and Eve contented herself by scrawling a line at the foot of Madge's letters, and sometimes with only a message. And long before we were ready to go home again, Mother got the news that Madge and Geoffrey Dagenham had made it up again and that Geoffrey was just as much at the Warren as he had been before Madge's last engagement. Father, who told her, said that he didn't think there was any idea of an engagement between the two, that they seemed friendly and that was all. "I think," he added, "that young Dagenham has had a lesson and has profited by it. As for Madge, she is looking quite herself again and seems to have forgotten the past altogether." "So," said my mother to me, "when we go home again, dear child, be sure that you don't do or say anything which will in any way remind Madge of what has gone by."

"But," said I, "supposing Oscar Devereux comes back again?"

"I don't think Oscar Devereux will come back again," said my mother, in a tone of conviction; "but in any case, the less it is talked about the better, and indeed, I don't want Madge to be reminded of her affair with him in any way whatever."

However, for once the Colonel turned out to be utterly wrong, for when we got back again to the Warren—I feeling ever so strong and well—we found Geoffrey Dagenham just on the old terms, and Madge apparently very well satisfied that it should be so. Really everything seemed just as it used to be before Madge went and got herself mixed up with that horrid black and yellow Mr. Devereux. Geoffrey Dagenham must have been very forgiving, or else her explanations must have been very satisfying, for he never by word or look alluded to the past in any shape or form, and during the early summer weather, when the roses were all in bloom and the Warren was looking its very best, Geoffrey and my sister were married.

They were married quite quietly, Madge wearing a pretty white walking-dress and a little white straw bonnet, trimmed with a cluster of white roses. Very charming she looked, very happy, and Geoffrey Dagenham was simply radiant, and so, as the Colonel said, with a great sigh of relief, "*That* is all happily settled and done with!" And then he looked at Mother and Mother smiled back at him, and somehow, none of us so much as thought of shedding a single tear over an event which was a very great delight even to the youngest of us.

So summer passed over. After a long honeymoon spent on the Continent, Madge and Geoffrey came back to their own home, though really, they seemed to be always at the Warren on some excuse or another. And then, as the autumn crept on I somehow got ill again and I was once more bundled off to a climate where I could get more sunshine than is possible in England at that time of year.

We did not go back to the same place, for Eve went this time, as Mother and the Colonel thought that it would be good for her to have a winter in a French-speaking country. The boys were all at school now, and Madge agreed to have them at Dagenham for the holidays, so the Warren was let to some one who wanted to be in Minchester for the hunting, and we were soon all settled down in a little white villa not very far from Cannes. This really was our life for the next four years. Tom went into the army, and Dick, by his own desire, went into business and had become quite a fashionable young man in London, or what seemed so to us. Charlie was at Marlborough and Frank was at a preparatory school and expected to make the change to Marlborough at Easter.

Now at this time, there was really little or nothing the matter with me. When I was in a warm climate and watched over by old Nurse, I seemed to ail nothing; but although I enjoyed the English summers the English autumns played terrible havoc with me. I became thin and transparent-looking, and my appetite fell off altogether; I was but a poor thing, and looked it. The moment that we got back to the shores of the Mediterranean, I began to mend; and so it fell out that during the next four years, we spent about six months of each one at or near Cannes

At this time, any idea of my being possessed of the second sight had been quite lost sight of by my family and in fact, by myself also. I was growing very fast, and was an awkward, gawky sort of girl, very much spoiled and petted by my father, whose favourite I was, as far as he permitted himself to have a favourite amongst us—for surely, never was a man more truly fond of all his children than the Colonel was of us. But nothing unpleasant happened, the past was never alluded to by any of us, and it was not until I was between fifteen and sixteen that my strange power once more declared itself.

CHAPTER VI.
MR. WARRENDER'S DIAMOND STAR.

The word that once escapes the tongue cannot be recalled; as the arrow cannot be detained which has once sped from the bow. —METASTASIO.

Oftentimes to win us to our harm The instruments of darkness tell us truths; Win us with honest trifles, to betray us In deepest consequence.
—*Macbeth*

WE had not been very long back from Cannes. The Warren had been thoroughly renovated during our absence, the man who had had it that winter having left at the end of March. It was the middle of May before we returned from the South, and under Madge's supervision the entire house had been re-papered and painted, so that everything looked very spick and span for our home-coming. Almost immediately after we had settled down, Tom came home on a fortnight's leave, accompanied by a great friend, a brother officer. There was very little for them to do, beyond the attraction of the Minchester May races, but they organised several rat hunts and pursuits of such-like small game. The men went to the races every day as long as they lasted, and we went over to Dagenham whenever they had nothing to do and played tennis on the asphalted courts, and in the evening there was generally something going on. There were a couple of concerts while Tom was at home and two new pieces at the theatre. Then we all dined at Dagenham, and several times Geoffrey and Madge came over and dined at the Warren, so that on the whole, we had as gay a time as anyone could expect to have in an ordinary country town at that particular season of the year.

It happened one night, when Madge and Geoffrey had come over, that after dinner we got playing silly games just as we had been used to do when we were all children. Among other things, we were playing that ridiculous game of "Consequences," all crowding round the dining-room table and scribbling away as if for dear life—what *he* said, what *she* said, what the *world* said, and what the consequences were. You know the game, of course. By some chance I happened to find myself next to Tom's friend, Mr. Warrender. I had just written down an adjective—as a matter of fact, it was the word "squinting"—and having turned down the edge of the sheet of paper, passed it on to my left hand neighbour, who happened to be Geoffrey Dagenham, and when I put out my right hand to receive the paper from Mr. Warrender he teasingly tried to keep it from me. However, he eventually let me have it, and I added the name of a man in the neighbourhood well known to us all. The next time his paper passed to me, he again tried to keep it from me, and again, and again, until we got right down the list of necessary remarks as far as the one which tells "what the world said." When I held out my hand to receive the paper from him, he made the usual pretence of withholding it from me, and caught hold of my hand. I daresay he thought it was very funny for so young a girl as I, but I only thought it rather silly. I meant to have the paper and was holding on to it like grim death, when he said to me, laughingly—"I wonder what your consequences will be, Miss Nancy?"

"Well, not the same as yours are," I replied.

"How do you know what my consequences are? I haven't written them myself yet," he said.

I really don't know what came over me—a sort of feeling as of electricity, a something passing from his hand, as it were through the paper and into my arm, a horrid sensation.

"You ought not to let him do it," I said warningly. "It is such a pretty star. Why should you let him take the stones out?"

"The stones? What do you mean?" he stammered.

"Why, that star, you know—the diamond star, Don't you know, there's a man in uniform picking the stones out of it, he is pushing them out with his penknife."

In his surprise, he pushed his chair back and stared at me with wide-open eyes indicative of the utmost consternation and surprise, as also were his parted lips.

"What on earth *are* you thinking about?" he asked.

In our surprise, the paper which we had both been holding fell on to the table.

"I don't know," I answered vaguely. "You asked me something about it. It was a star."

"But how did you see that? Tell me, what do you know about a star?"

"I don't know anything," I answered.

"What made you say that to me just now?"

"I don't know," I replied, "it came somehow. Have you lost a diamond star?"

"Of course, I have. But surely Tom told you all about it?"

"Not a word!" said Tom, from the other side of the table. "I say, Nancy, you are at your old tricks again."

"My tricks!" I looked round the ring of eager faces and met my father's penetrating gaze.

"Miss Nancy," said Mr. Warrender, turning into his chair and looking at me searchingly, "did something in your brain tell you of that star which I lost?"

"Yes, I suppose so. You have lost a star, haven't you?"

"Of course, I have. Not only that, but my servant is actually under arrest at the present moment for stealing it and he stoutly denies all knowledge of it. Are you sure you didn't hear anything about it?"

"Perfectly certain."

"Do you mind taking hold of my hand and seeing if the knowledge comes back to you?"

Of course, I took hold of his hand, and almost immediately the impression of a bare, ill-furnished room came to me.

"Now, tell me what you see?" he said imploringly.

His voice sounded far, far away and the entire room in which we were sitting seemed to have gone from me. "I see a square room with two small windows in it," I replied. "It has a square carpet in the middle with a green border. There is only one nice picture in the room—it is The Huguenots,' the one where the girl is tying a white band round her lover's arm."

"Yes, go on!" said he eagerly.

"There is a little bed in one corner covered by a fur rug and some crimson pillows at one end—or perhaps it is a sofa. There are some pegs on the wall with some belts and a forage cap with a gold border, and a row of boots on a sort of cupboard on one side of the fire-place. On the other side of the room, opposite to the bed is a chest of drawers, very plain with brass handles. I see a gentleman come into the room—oh, yourself! You walk up to the fireplace and are standing filling your pipe, then you strike a match and light it. Now you are sitting down in the big chair, which has arms made of broad straps with brass hooks to lower or raise them. You are reading a letter and you put it down and hang your arm over the side of the chair as if you were very tired, and at last you look up and there is a little clock on one corner of the mantel-shelf—the mantel-shelf has a fringe round it and brass nails—and you haul yourself up as if you were dead beat. Now you are going out of the room. There—you have shut the door, the room is empty, the room is quite empty—somebody is coming! A man enters, a red-haired man—"

"That is Mason," I heard him say across the table to Tom.

"He has his hair cut very short, and he is wearing a tan-coloured suit. He seems to be a servant, for he tidies up the room and then he fills his pipe out of the tobacco jar and he lights a match just as you did. Now he is going. There is nobody in the room, again it is quite empty. Stay—the door opens again, very gently, somebody looks in, a man with black hair, and a black moustache trained to a spike on either side. He has a big blue ring on his finger. He comes in, looks round, shuts the door behind him, goes to the mantel-shelf, reads some of the letters, fills his pipe, but not out of the jar on the mantel-shelf. He smells that and puts it down with a gesture of disgust. He has a little pouch in his pocket with a monogram worked in coloured silks on one side of it, he fills his pipe from that and lights it from a box of matches on the mantel-shelf. Then he looks round the room, takes some keys out of his pocket, tries the drawer, opens it, takes a case out of it, locks the drawer again, puts the keys back in his pocket—the pocket is in the breast of his tunic, he is in undress uniform—then he walks across the room, back to the fireplace again. He opens the case, which is still in his hand. There is a diamond star in it. He drops the case into the middle of the fire. It is burnt up in a moment. Then he quietly sits down and seems to be picking the stones out of the star——It is all gone! I can't see any more!" I ended.

In an instant the whole vision had faded away and I was once more sitting at the table in the dining-room at the Warren with a dozen eager faces all turned towards me.

"This is perfectly awful!" said Mr. Warrender, looking across the table at Tom. "Are you sure you never said anything about it to your sister?"

"My dear chap, didn't we agree not to speak of it? Didn't we agree, the day we came down here, that we would not mention it at all?" said Tom, without hesitation.

"Yes, but I didn't know whether you might have forgotten that."

"I swear to you that I haven't breathed a word about it to anybody, not even to the Colonel here. Nancy has been at her old tricks. Nancy is right enough. My dear chap, you have only got one course to follow—go back and take your man from under arrest at once, and put the guilt on to the person to whom it is due.

"But, my dear Tom, you can't think that——"

"You had better not mention any names," said Tom, leaning his elbow on the table and biting his knuckles, which was a habit Tom had when he was at all excited or worried. "I've not said a word, I tell you; I haven't seen Nancy alone for more than a year. When I was at home last on anything like a long leave, the man that she described to you to-night was not in the regiment."

"Is that so?"

"If I remember rightly, Mother, you came home a month earlier last year than you did this?"

"Yes," said Mother, "that is quite true."

"And I spent about three weeks here."

"Yes, so you did."

"I tell you I haven't seen Nancy alone since, and that man only came into the regiment last June or July. Nancy knows nothing whatever about him. I have got something else to do than to write home long descriptions of my brother officers or of their quarters, or even what transpires in the regiment. There never was a worse letter writer than I am. I daresay my mother can show you a good many letters of mine that begin and end on one page, and as for you, Sir," looking at Father, "my epistles to you are even more businesslike than that."

"My dear Tom," said the Colonel, "your epistles to me generally consist of this—'Dear Colonel, can you send me ten pounds and oblige your affectionate son, Thomas Reynard?'"

"But I can't think," cried Mr. Warrender, still with the same frank unbelief—

"You needn't think at all," broke in Tom, "it isn't necessary for you to think. This doesn't surprise any of *us* Nancy has seen things before, much more serious even than this matter of your diamond star. What Nancy sees in that extraordinary second-sight sort of way you may depend upon as being absolutely correct. You have only got one course, my dear chap—go back to-morrow, tell the Colonel everything, tax the man with it, set your servant free. You will find that you will probably get your diamonds back and there will be a change in the regiment just about as soon as you can say 'Jack Robinson!' "

"But what is the meaning of it?" said the Colonel. "Have you lost a diamond star?"

"Colonel Reynard," said Tom's friend, "it is like this. We gave some private theatricals a short time ago for the benefit of the Soldiers' Institute at Danford. I had to play the part of Charles I.—yes, I admit it was a very ambitious thing to do, but we took it into our heads we would do Charles I., and we got the necessary permission and we did it—more or less badly, I need hardly explain to you. Among other things, it was necessary that I should wear a diamond star, and a lady—the wife of one of the officers—lent me one. I didn't have the opportunity of returning it to her the same evening, and the next day it disappeared out of my despatch box in my chest of drawers, which is the usual thing you see in a man's quarters. My servant admitted having been in the room between my going to afternoon stables and round the teas, and coming back for some tea and toast, which I had that day in my own quarters. When I went away, the star was there, and when I came back, it was gone. Naturally, suspicion pointed to the servant and he has been in cells ever since."

"And you may bet your very life," said Tom, leaning back in his chair and thrusting his hands deep down into his trouser-pockets, "that the poor chap never touched the star, and that the other one did. I always had my suspicions of that fellow, Warrender, always."

"But do you mean to say," put in the Colonel, in a voice that was an odd mixture of indignation and curiosity, "that Nancy's description of the man who took the star tallies with that of one of your brother officers?"

"In every respect," said young Warrender deliberately.

"Tallies as a photograph tallies with its original," put in Tom, with conviction.

At this point, Geoffrey came into the conversation—"I say, old chap," said he, speaking across the table to Tom, "what made you say that Nancy was at her old tricks again?"

Tom looked at Madge, who turned a vivid guilty scarlet, the first time I had ever seen my sister flush painfully in the whole of my life. I perceived in an instant that she had never told him the whole story of her engagement to Oscar Devereux. I was greatly surprised, because ever since they had been married, I had always believed Madge to be utterly wrapped up in her husband, and would not have credited her with being able to keep even the smallest thing back from him. Yet, evidently, she had kept back this whole story, had kept it absolutely to herself.

"Why, of course," Tom began, "it was Nancy that showed up——" and then I think somebody's foot must have conveyed a hint to him that he had better stop, for he broke off short and after looking round the table bit his words off with an embarrassed laugh—"Really, Nancy, old lady, I must apologize to you for discussing you in this way," he said to me, and very awkwardly he said it, "don't let's talk about it any more. I will tell you by and by, Warrender. It's rather a sore subject with the young lady!"

It was all very well of Tom to put it all on to me and say that it was a sore subject to me when, as a matter of fact, it was not. I was not in the least touchy or sore about my occasional power of giving impressions. However, for Madge's sake, I didn't mind being given away so unmercifully so long as Geoffrey's attention was taken entirely off the subject.

Later on, when he and Madge had gone home—indeed, after I had gone to bed—Tom came into my room and sat down on the edge of my bed to talk things over.

"I say, Nancy, old lady," he began, "you really *did* see all that to-night, didn't you?"

"Yes, I suppose so," I answered. "I don't see it now, if that is what you mean."

"How do these things happen to you?"

"I don't know," I replied. "When it comes to me, I tell it. It has to come out. I couldn't keep it to myself. Beyond that I cannot tell you anything."

"But do you really see things?"

"I suppose so. Yes, I certainly have the impression that I see them."

"Well, you have made it very awkward for that chap, you know."

"I can't help that," I answered, "he shouldn't steal diamond stars."

"No, that is true enough. I think I shall go up with Warrender to-morrow and see the thing through. Of course, it is awfully rough luck for the poor chap who has been in the cells all these days on account of it. As I said to Warrender at the time, it is all owing to the poor devil having red hair. Somehow people who have red hair always get suspected of every villainy under the sun, and this poor beggar has got the reddest hair you ever saw in your life! It is carrot-coloured. Not that I like red-haired people," my brother went on reflectively. "By Jove, I would not marry a red headed woman——"

"My dear Tom," said I, "I should hope you are not going to marry any kind of woman, red-headed or green-headed, or with any other coloured head that you like to mention. Why, you haven't got sense enough, my dear boy, to keep your feet out of the most awful trap you can possibly think of! Why, you nearly gave Madge away to Geoffrey to-night!"

"Well, now, how on earth was I to know she had never told Geoffrey a word about it?"

"What made you stop as you did?" I asked.

"I don't know, but I had a kick which I should say I shall feel for a week!"

"It couldn't have been Madge," I said with a laugh.

"Oh, no, it wasn't Madge, she was too far away. I think it was the Governor. By Jove, it *was* a shinning! Still, it's nothing to what will happen to-morrow, speaking metaphorically."

"What will be the result?" I asked.

"Oh, for—? oh, by the bye, I had better not tell anybody who it was, not even you. I expect it will be hushed up, you know. He will have to give up the star and clear out of the regiment. It would never do to have a scandal about it. He will just have to go. But, by Jove, I wouldn't stand in that fellow's shoes for something!"

CHAPTER VII.
THE NAMELESS ONE.

Do not imagine that a fault is amended when it is merely onfessed.
—WHATHLY.

With aching hands and bleeding feet We dig and heap, lay stone on stone; We bear the burden and the heat Of the long day, and wish 'twere done :— Nor till the hours of light return All we have built do we discern. —MATTHEW ARNOLD.

EARLY on the following day my brother Tom and his guest, Mr. Warrender, went off to Danford, where their regiment was quartered. We had quite an early breakfast and we all got up for it, but nobody said very much about my vision of the previous evening, probably because Mr. Warrender had really believed in Tom's awkward assertion that my gift was a sore point with me and that I should be better pleased if it was not talked about and discussed. "I expect we shall be back by eight o'clock, Mother," said Tom, just as they were about to start.

"I suppose you will try to catch the five fifteen train," put in the Colonel.

"Yes, if we get through this business," Tom replied.

"Well, that does not get into Minchester till eight thirty-seven," said my father, who always carried a little local time-table in some convenient pocket, to the great comfort of his family and acquaintances.

"In that case," said Mother, "we will make dinner at nine. It will prevent you finding an uneatable meal if you do catch that train."

"Thank you so much, Mrs. Reynard," said Mr. Warrender. "I really feel that I am giving you a tremendous lot of trouble, but I am afraid I cannot help myself in this particular instance."

"Oh, no trouble at all," said my mother easily; "and even if you did give me a very great deal of trouble, I would not grudge it to save a poor fellow from being unjustly accused, especially a soldier too." And then they had to rush off and tear down the road as fast as they could go, or, as Tom put it, "just bolt as quick as they could- lay legs to ground."

When they had fairly gone we four—Father, Mother, Eve and I—went back to the table to finish our breakfast. After a moment's silence, the Colonel looked across the table at Mother. "Blanche," he remarked, in a tone of some surprise—"did you know that Madge had kept all that about Devereux from Geoffrey?"

"Well, yes, I did," Mother replied; "in fact, Sep, she spoke to me about it at the time of the renewal of the engagement, and when I found what an insuperable objection she had to speaking of Oscar Devereux to anyone and to Greoffrey most of all, I advised her to make it a condition with him that they left that subject alone for ever. I daresay I ought to have warned all the others, but it never occurred to me that anyone would think of alluding to it, and you know, sometimes when one has specially warned people off dangerous ground, it seems to create the strongest desire to drag that one matter into their conversation."

"Yes, yes, you are quite right, my dear, as you generally are," said the Colonel easily. "And of course, no one would have expected Tom or anyone else to be such a complete fool as to allude to so delicate a matter before strangers. It was lucky that I was near enough to stop Master Tom before he bad time to go any further."

"Oh, was it you that gave Tom that kick?" I exclaimed.

"Yes, but how did you know anything about it?" my father asked.

"Tom came into my room last night, and he told me that some one had almost broken his leg. Oh, he wasn't vindictive about it," I added with a laugh.

"I should hope not," rejoined the Colonel in an amused tone. "Of course, I'm sorry if I hurt the lad—hurting my youngsters is not much in my line and never was. But at a moment like that, one cannot stop to think out a gentle reminder; one has only one object, to change the subject. I must apologise to poor old Tom when they come back again. By Jove, what a devil of a row there will be when they explain matters to Le Merchant."

But when the two boys did come back they seemed altogether disinclined to talk about what had happened during the day. They were both tired out and said that they wanted their dinner beyond all things. So we let them eat in peace though we were all simply dying to hear what the upshot had been. And at last, when the two servants had gone out of the room and Father had handed the cigarettes round, they gratified our very natural curiosity.

It was Tom who began the disclosure. "I say," he began half-hesitatingly, "I've promised and vowed all sorts of things in all of your names. We settled that business, and Colonel Le Merchant wanted us both to promise that we would not breathe a single word of what had taken place to any living soul. But, as I represented to him, that was all very well, but the truth had come out through my sister, and I was bound to satisfy her that she had not been making mistakes and perhaps putting everyone on the wrong track. So, as the old chap saw the reasonableness of that, I eased his mind by promising that I would bind you all down to secrecy before I gave you a single detail of what took place at Danford to-day. I suppose you are all perfectly ready to give such a promise?"

We all declared our willingness to comply with this very reasonable requirement, and then Tom did his tale unfold.

"Well, Warrender and I got to Danford soon after eleven o'clock and went straight to the orderly-room to see if the Chief happened to be there and disengaged. He was there, apparently up to his eyes in work—you know, sir, how a Commanding-officer can surround himself with all the evidences of a toil-worn and laborious life, though I don't think it is necessary for me to explain to you what make-believe most of it is, or what a show-figure the Commanding-officer usually is."

Tom paused here in a most effective sort of way; and Mr. Warrender looked up as if he expected a perfect storm of indignant denial from our father. However, if that really was what he expected, all I can say is that it didn't come off. Father puffed ,away at his cigarette in the most perfect good-humour and waited for Tom's story. He was used to that kind of chaff, and indeed had encouraged it in every one of us ever since we could toddle. Tom, finding that the Colonel was not to be drawn this time, went on with his story.

"He looked rather surprised to see us and asked what had brought us? And really, when you come to think of it, it must have been a startler for him, particularly as he had made such an awful fuss over giving us our poor little scrap of leave from the delights of soldiering. I gave a hint to Warrender, and Warrender dug his elbow into my ribs as an inducement to me to go ahead and get the whole matter over as soon as possible. 'The fact is, Colonel,' I said, finding that Warrender was determined to shove everything on to me—'we have a very important communication to make to you and if you could spare us a few minutes alone—'

" 'Certainly—certainly—' the Chief replied promptly. 'Er—er—Mr. Villebois, we can finish that little matter presently. Orderly, you can go. I'll send for you by and by.'

"As the two went out of the room," Tom continued, "the Chief sat in his chair and looked at us. 'Now,' he said, 'what is this business?'

"I simply cannot tell you," my brother went on, "the effect of my story on the Colonel. Really, I thought more than once that the poor old chap was going to have a fit on the spot. 'This must be kept quiet,' he said, and he was regularly shaking, as if *he* had had a hand in the affair. 'We cannot have it said that such a thing happened in the old 26th; the regiment would never get over it, never. Gentlemen, this must go no farther. Even the suspicion that one of my officers could be thought capable of taking the property of another must not be allowed to creep out into the world. But, of course, I can give no opinion until Mr.—we can call him Mr. X—, for convenience sake—has heard what you have to say.'

"And by the bye," Tom went on after a moment's pause, "I promised the Chief that in any case I would not divulge the name to a living soul. Warrender, you too made the same promise."

"I did," said Mr. Warrender.

"Anyway," Tom continued, "the Chief sent for the man—the one that you saw, Nancy—and said he required his presence in the office immediately. In a very few minutes he came. 'You sent for me, Sir,' he said inquiringly; then looked at us 'Ah, you back again?' he remarked, 'good-morning.'

" 'Mr. X—,' said the Chief, in his most heavy father style of voice, 'I sent for you to give you an opportunity of hearing something that has come to my knowledge this morning. You will not have forgotten that Mr. Warrender here lost a diamond star under somewhat unusual circumstances a short time ago. Mr. Warrender has reason to believe that you were the person who took it. Have you anything to say in the matter?'

"I never," Tom went on, "saw a man so struck all of a heap in my life. He turned and glared at Warrender as if he would just have killed him then and there if he had dared to do it. 'Mr. Warrender says that *I* took his star?' he blurted out. 'Then why did Mr. Warrender permit his servant to be arrested and to be under arrest now, unless I am very much mistaken?'

" 'That is not the question, Sir,' thundered the Chief, in an awful voice. 'The only question with which you have anything to do is this—did you or did you not take the star?'

" ' Sir, you insult me,' the other burst out.

" 'Not intentionally. It cannot be more painful to you to be asked such a question than it is for me to have to ask it,' the Chief replied, promptly.

'But I think you had better tell Mr. X—exactly what happened last evening.'

"I did so," Tom went on, "I repeated every little detail of your vision just as you told it to us, and then X—stood up and gave an unqualified denial to everything. Warrender and I were perfectly nonplussed, for the fellow put it to the Chief in such a plausible way that it sounded real enough.

'I ask you, Sir,' he said, in the most reasonable tone in the world, 'what on earth would be the good of a diamond star or any other star to me? I am more than rich enough to buy fifty such things if I needed them. But I don't need them. I have no earthly use for them. Besides, it would be absurd to blast a man's whole career on no better authority than the sickly fancy of an hysterical young girl. I think I have heard you say, Reynard, that your young sister has had to winter in the South of France for several years?' which, of course, I was obliged to admit was the case.

"However, I began to feel, the more the fellow explained things away, that I was right and that he had taken the star, whether he actually had any need of it or not. So I put just one little spoke in his wheel which had the effect of completely changing the general aspect of affairs. 'There is just one thing that I should like to say, Sir,' I remarked to the Chief. 'You see, Sir, I feel that I am somewhat responsible, the seer of this strange vision being my sister. X—might imagine that Mr. Warrender and I had freely talked of the loss of his star, but in truth such is not the case. We have never once mentioned it, and I will positively swear that I have not once mentioned Mr. X—'s name to any member of my family, I have never described him or in any way given what might have been the clue to this vision. Now, I only wish to ask one thing. It is this: Of course, Mr. X—will have no objection to having his quarters and belongings searched by some suitable person.'

"X—bounced up like a parched pea on a hot shovel," Tom continued. " 'Certainly not, I will submit to no such insult,' he blazed out.

" 'Then, of course, we shall have no choice but to think that you *cannot*—that you are afraid to give that satisfaction.'

" 'If you order it to be done, Sir,' he began, when the Chief interrupted him gravely and quietly: 'I could not order any such thing, Mr. X—,' he said. 'But as your commanding officer and as your best friend in this matter, I strongly advise you to willingly and cheerfully embrace such an excellent chance of satisfying everybody concerned in this miserable affair.'

"The effect of the Chiefs quiet words was almost miraculous," Tom went on. "I never could have believed that such a change could have come over any man in the course of a few minutes as came over X—while the Colonel was speaking. He dropped down on the nearest chair and hid his face on his arms. 'Mr. X—' exclaimed the Chief in a tone of the utmost surprise, 'what is the meaning of this?'

"He raised his head at last, and looked wildly at us all. 'What does it mean?' he cried, 'Why, that I can't hold out any longer. I did take Warrender's star. Why? Oh, why do any of us do crazy things? I don't know why. Now what are you going to do? To send for the police, or what?'

" 'Mr. X—,' said the Chief, 'I am not going to send for the police. I am going to do nothing which will in any way let this disgraceful story creep out beyond the ears of those who are most nearly concerned. You will, of course, restore the star to Mr. Warrender.'

" 'Yes,' answered X—sullenly. 'Here are my keys, you can go and fetch it.'

" 'Not at all,' put in the Colonel sharply, 'we will go and find it together, all of us. Then you will hand over to me a suitable sum of money as compensation for the man who has been lying in the cells suspected of your crime. After that you will send in your papers and you will leave the Service without delay. Of course, you will not enter the Mess-rooms again.'

"Poor beggar," said Tom quite sympathetically, "I give you my word that I was never so sorry for any human being in the whole of my life. He seemed so crushed and down-trodden. I pitied him with all my heart."

"And I," echoed Mr. Warrender.

"He agreed to everything," Tom continued; "he handed over a tenner for Warrender's servant, went with us to get the star, which had suffered a good bit by the change of keepers, for he had punched nearly all the stones out and the setting was bent here and there and a good deal marked and scratched by the pen-knife which he had used for the purpose. 'You will pay for having it put right, of course,' said the Chief, who was perfectly pitiless in his anger and disgust. *He* had no pity whatever for the chap, not a bit of it.

"And then we all went back to the Orderly-room, and we all of us swore that we would never divulge a word of what had happened, and then he was told that he could go. It was after that," Tom ended, "that I promised that I would not say one single word about the matter until I had first got your promise to keep absolute silence about it for ever."

As Tom ceased speaking my father drew a long breath. "H'm, it's one of the strangest stories I ever heard. Heaven be thanked that such a thing never happened in my regiment. I don't believe that I should have been half as judicious as your Chief, on my word I don't. But my dear child," turning and laying his hand on mine, "what a regular little fire-brand you are. We shall have to beware of you, my dear."

"Miss Nancy, I wonder if you could find out for me where my chestnut mare is—I lost a valuable mare about a year ago. Perhaps Miss Nancy could give me the clue to that also."

He held out his hand to me as he spoke, but my father hurriedly made mine a prisoner within his own. "No, no, I strongly object to that," he exclaimed. "I don't want Nancy to encourage her power; it is quite inconvenient enough as it is. Besides that, Nancy is but a delicate slip of a girl, and the less this sort of thing grows on her the better. Remember, Nancy, my precious, that I wish you never to experiment in any way."

CHAPTER VIII.
"THAT'S MY BROTHER."

Full of hope and and yet of heart-break. —*Hiawatha.*

There are things of which I may not speak, There are dreams that cannot die, There are thoughts that make the strong heart weak, And bring a pallor to the cheek And a mist into the eye. —*My Lost Youth.*

WHAT Tom called his "little scrap of leave" soon came to an end, and then he and Mr. Warrender went back to their regiment and we heard no more about the affair of the diamond star. True to our trust, we never spoke of it or alluded to it in any way, and nobody outside our immediate family circle knew that the incident had even taken place.

Several times during the rest of his stay, Mr. Warrender tried his best to induce me to try if I could not find some clue or trace of the mare which had been stolen from him a year previously; but though, after many refusals and reminders that the Colonel would be exceedingly angry if he knew that I had been deliberately experimenting with my strange power, I at last let myself be over-persuaded and did let him hold my hand for a few minutes, yet no vision of any kind came to me and for all the trace of a mare that I saw, the young man might never have been possessed of any kind of a gee in the whole of his life.

"No, it is evidently no use, Mr. Warrender," I said, as I took my hand away. "What I can see I can see, and it is no use trying to force it."

"But you needn't take your hand away, Nancy," he said reproachfully. "It won't hurt you to leave it for a little while where it was very comfortable."

I laughed outright. "It was not so very comfortable, Mr. Warrender," I replied.

"No?" in a deeply hurt tone. "Ah, you're a hard-hearted little soul, Nancy, and I'm a great ass to set any value on your good opinion."

He got up from the garden seat on which we were sitting and walked away with his hands in his pockets, I looking after him ruefully enough. "There now, he is vexed because I could not find out anything about his stupid mare," my thoughts ran. "As if I could help it. But there, if he likes to upset himself about nothing, he must just be upset. *I* can't help it."

Mr. Warrender, however, did not seem to be at all upset when we met again, and if he was not quite as gay and free and easy as usual, very few people would have noticed any difference in him. I fancy that he avoided me somewhat, but I did not dare to ask Eve, for Eve was a bit of a blab and I was afraid she might peach to the Colonel about my trying to see something of the lost mare. So during the few days that they were still at the Warren, I had to hold my tongue and say nothing. And at last they went away and the Warren settled down into its prosaic and ordinary ways again.

"Mrs. Keynard," Tom's friend said at parting, "I have to thank you for one of the most pleasant visits that I ever paid in my life. I hope you will ask me again some day."

"Why, of course we will," Mother answered in her kindest tones, "more especially when you are so easily pleased and satisfied with so very little. I never had anyone staying in the house who gave so little trouble as you have done, Mr. Warrender. Come back to us at any time when you have leave and want to have a quiet time in the country."

But Mr. Warrender never did come back to the Warren and I never saw him again. Leave was very difficult to get that summer, for the regiment was worked tremendously hard, and when Tom did get a few days, he spent them in Town and I suppose his great chum went with him. At all events, he did not come to us. They both had their long leave the following winter when we were at Cannes, which the Colonel liked better than any foreign town he had ever been in—I believe because he was able to gamble a little, a pursuit at which he generally contrived to win. We had scarcely got settled again at the Warren before Tom sent a telegram saying that he was coming home for a few hours and would we send a trap to the station to meet him? Of course we did; indeed the Colonel went himself to fetch him from the train—I really believe because he thought Tom had got into some scrape and he could not wait till he reached the house to hear what it was. But poor dear Tom had not got into a scrape at all, for Tom was a real good boy, though not a bit soppy or anything of that kind. No, it was not Tom who had got into a scrape but the whole nation, for he brought the news that there was what he called "a devil of a shindy out in India" and the 26th had been ordered off at once at something like three days' notice. "I tore up to Town last night," Tom told us, "and ordered as much as I could in the time—no fancy things you know, sir, but just the merest necessaries for a hot climate. A good half the fellows are in a pretty corner, for the tradespeople don't see putting themselves out for anything but ready money, and very few of us have got a fiver to bless ourselves with. However, thank goodness, I'm pretty well off just now as it happens."

The Colonel was deeply interested in the "shindy" in the East. "I did hear something about it," he said, "but I expect it's only an ordinary kind of scare. They are always getting them up and then a few of the wise ones have the satisfaction of saying 'I told you so,' though where that particular pleasure or satisfaction comes is hard to tell. Still, of course, it's best to be on the safe side and not have the Mutiny game played over again. I always felt that it was such a pity that the troops out there did not foregather a little and that we did not make ourselves more to the natives socially. You know it really is deuced hard for them. The conquering race isn't content to be the conquering race, but it makes a point of seeking to ram that same fact down the throats of the native races at every turn. On my word, it is hard and I firmly believe it is the greatest mistake in all the world."

During this harangue my mother had been staring at Father with all her eyes. "Why, Sep!" she exclaimed, in tones of the utmost consternation, "when did all these new-fangled notions come to you? Have you forgotten about Mrs. Ramdejee?"

My Father had the grace to redden perceptibly under the calm gaze of Mother's serene eyes. "Yes, yes, I know all about that," he said rather uneasily. "But, of course, I thought very differently on those matters then; and even now, when I do see how short-sighted our policy has always been, I would not go so far as to mix the races in that way. No, no, certainly not."

"Tell us about Mrs. Ramdejee," cried Eve coaxingly.

"Oh, it was nothing," answered the Colonel half impatiently.

"Still, we want to know, every one of us," persisted Eve, who was a perfect bull-dog in never letting go of an idea when she had once got it.

"Well, Mrs. Ramdejee was a pretty English girl who came out to Lahmoor as governess to some children in the 92nd," the Colonel began. "And I suppose she had a pretty bad time, for Mrs. Lassalle was a plain and very jealous little body, with an idea that half the fellows in the station were in love with her—which they decidedly were not—and she was thoroughly disgusted at the governess, who had been sent out by her friends, turning out to be so very pretty, and in consequence she kept her entirely in the background. Eventually, this girl attracted the admiration of a young native barrister who had been educated in England, and she married him. I—I—well, I objected to your mother knowing them or meeting them, and——"

"But why," Eve asked in wonder.

"Oh, well nobody does, most people do object in India," said the Colonel rather lamely, "and I shared the same prejudices as the rest. But now, I feel that perhaps I was wrong and if I went out again I might feel differently."

At this point Tom said something very rude under his breath, something about pigs and flying and unlikely birds. I think Mother heard it, for she laughed softly to herself. Mother was quite alive to all Father's delightful inconsistencies, though she adored him.

"It does seem most bitterly unjust on the very face of it," the Colonel went on—" for us to treat the natives, to whom the soil should by right belong, as if they were dirt under our feet; and yet——"

"And yet if you were to go back again," put in Mother, quietly, "you would do exactly the same as you did before."

"I daresay I should," Father admitted.

"The fact is," said Tom wisely, "that a fellow has to do pretty much what all the other fellows do. If it's the swagger thing to refuse to meet natives outside of official houses, everyone who is anyone will go on refusing to meet them. If anyone is strong enough to set the fashion of making natives the fashion, and can do it without the cover of an official position, why then the custom of refusing to meet them will drop out."

"My dear lad," said the Colonel, "you've put the case in a nutshell."

Tom's few hours of leave were soon over and equally soon the wrench of parting was over. It was a wrench, although our boys had been away from home for years, and being a military family, we were all of us accustomed to think little or nothing of saying good bye. Still, for all that it was a wrench, for Tom, who was the dearest fellow in the world, was the first of all us youngsters who had said good-bye before taking so long a journey; and besides that there was trouble in the air, and we did not know to what danger and hardship he might be going. Of course, it might turn out to be a mere nothing, and we all hoped and prayed that it would do so. But, as the Colonel said, when thousands of natives all through a district take to breaking their cakes in a different way to that in which they have broken it from time im-memorial, why it generally means something, and anything that means something in India usually means something unpleasant.

Thus we watched Tom's progress with the gravest anxiety, far more so indeed than we should have done at any ordinary time. It followed the usual course of sol-diers on their way out to the gorgeous East. We heard from Gib., from Malta, Suez, Aden, and then from Bombay.

Tom himself was not at all concerned about the future. He wrote in the very best of spirits and his letters were for him laboriously long, that is to say he man-aged to fill three sides of the large thin paper on which he wrote. Among other items of information he told us that he had got all his things before sailing, that he had never felt a single qualm and that his friend Warrender had been in his berth all the way to Gib. and even part of the way to Malta. "Poor old chap!" Tom wrote, "when he did get up on deck, he looked like a ghost and he was so fearfully weak that he could scarcely stagger across the saloon. I don't know," he added, "how the poor old chap is going to stand a hot climate."

By the time the 26th reached Bombay the scare about the specially broken cakes was quite at an end, and, as Tom said, they might just as well have been given time to get suitable clothing and necessaries, instead of being bundled out of Eng-land with scarcely an extra set of shirts among them. "However," Tom wrote cheer-fully, "on the whole, most of the fellows have a great deal to be thankful for. Half of them were in a blue funk about their bills, not knowing how they would get out of England without being arrested for debt. As it is, they all slipped away very neatly, and no possible blame to them. And as the regiment won't be back for ten years, it's a bad look-out for the tailors."

After all, I don't suppose that all the officers of the 26th put together owed such a lot of money, and probably they had spent so much during the previous ten years that the tradesmen would not care very much whether they lost what was owing or not. Tom, who did not owe any bills, continued to write home most cheerfully, only his letters grew shorter and shorter and with every one more like the letters he had written from school, from Sandhurst, and from his regiment.

They had been out about six months when I gathered some news which Tom never meant us to know. It happened that Mother and I were sitting working together, when we heard the double knock of the postman. I ran out and fetched the letters from the box.

"Three for the Colonel," I remarked. "Two for Eve and one for you. One from Tom."

"Read it to me, dear," said Mother, who was nursing a bad cold and had neuralgia, on account of which she was sitting very near to the fire with her head wrapped up in a fine white Shetland shawl.

"It's the usual half sheet," I said with a laugh; then began to read. "My dear Mother——" and then a sort of mist came over me and I said——"Stop! You're not to do that. That's my brother——Oh——Oh——Tom, wake up, wake up, he is going to kill you. Tom! Tom!"

I was conscious of Mother's voice speaking in very decided accents.

"Nancy, what is it? Nancy, speak!"

I saw distinctly a room with high white walls and with very little furniture. The principal thing was a bed which stood almost in the middle of the room and which was hung with white curtains all round.

They were very thin and you could see through them. There was a chair or two and a dressing table set out with all the brushes and toilet things that a man uses, and at one side was a photograph of Mother in a smart silver frame. The floor was covered with matting and a big dog was lying near the bed. As I was watching I saw a man, a native, in white clothing, come stealthily into the room and go towards the dog, which raised its head and growled at him, just lifting its heavy lip so as to show its teeth. The man had a cloth in his hand, apparently a damp cloth, and this by a dexterous movement he flung over the dog's head and then threw himself upon him. In a minute or so the great brown animal ceased to struggle, and then the man moved softly towards the bed and gently drew the curtain aside. To my horror I saw that he had a knife in his hand and I then shrieked out aloud—" No, no, you mustn't do it. That's Tom! Tom! Oh, do wake up. Ah—h, he has struck him! Oh, coward! ***Coward!***"—and then I hid my face in my hands and burst into a storm of passionate tears.

CHAPTER IX.
A GHASTLY STORY.

They have sown the wind, and shall reap the whirlwind. —HOSEA.

Faint not, and fret not, for threatened woe, Watchman, on Truth's grey height! Few though the faithful, and fierce though the foe, Weakness is aye Heaven's might. —NEWMAN.

WHEN I came round to myself again, Mother was standing by me, her arm round me and her head pressed hard against mine. No, I do not mean that I fainted, but my grief was uncontrollable and I was almost in hysterics.

"My dear, my dear, what was it? What did you see?" she cried, holding me fast.

"Oh Mother," I gasped—I was shivering with what I had seen, but I contrived to repeat it all to her. She heard me to the end, her face growing whiter with every moment.

"My child," she said in a shaking voice, "do you think that by any chance you can have been deceived? You have not been very well, and for some time past we have been anxious about our dear boy: do you think it possible that your nerves or senses have played you false and that your strange power has gone a little astray?"

"I don't know, Mother," I replied, "it all seemed so horridly real and I saw the man raise the knife—Oh," and then I broke off shuddering again.

My mother put Tom's letter into my hand again.

"I know that your father does not wish you to make experiments with this power of yours, but this is a time when you may fairly try your utmost to find out the truth. Hold the letter again and try to see what happened after the man struck Tom."

I obeyed at once, but though I tried with might and main, with all my heart and soul, to see what else had happened to our dear boy, my mind remained perfectly blank and not the slightest trace of a vision came to illumine the darkness which what I had seen had cast over us.

We were still sitting in the firelit room when the Colonel and my two sisters came in. Geoffrey Dagenham had gone up to Town for a few days on business and Madge was spending a few days at home. They had all been to an afternoon party in Minchester and came in laughing and chatting gaily together.

"Well, my love," said the Colonel as he opened the door, "and how is the cold? Any better?"

"Sep!" said Mother—just that one word. But Father understood—he always did understand Mother; he could read her like a book.

He caught hold of her. "What is it?" he asked. Then he perceived the letters lying on the table and, recognising Tom's handwriting, he stretched out his hand and picked his up.

Mother found her voice. "That's nothing," she said; "it is quite an ordinary letter; but Nancy was reading it and she has seen something. Oh Sep, Sep! My boy, my dear boy?"

I scarcely know how we managed to tell him all that I had seen, but we did it somehow. He sat like a man turned to stone for a few minutes, while Eve, who was excessively fond of Tom, hid her face against the chimney-shelf, and Madge broke out into bitter weeping.

"Oh, Nannie, Nannie," she cried, "are you quite sure that it was Tom you saw? Could it have been anyone else?"

"It was Tom," I answered. "I saw him distinctly."

"You don't think that you've been dwelling on him lately, and so your mind has played you tricks."

She was crying bitterly and could scarcely frame the words for her sobs.

"My dear Madge," I replied, "I have not been thinking any more of Tom than usual. I only told what I saw; I didn't **want** to see it—why should I?"

There was a moment's silence and then my sister gave a long sigh, "Nancy is always right in what she sees," she said, hopelessly.

At this point the Colonel looked up and spoke to Mother. "Blanche," he said, "I shall go into the town at once and wire out to Le Merchant. We cannot go on in this suspense until we hear in the ordinary way."

"Oh, Sep, if you only will," Mother cried in despairing tones.

He went to her writing table and wrote out the telegram. "I think this will do," he said—"Le Merchant, 26th Hussars, Sialkote, India. Is my son well?—Reynard."

"Yes," said Mother anxiously. "Then we shall know the worst at once. Nancy has tried and tried and she can see nothing else."

I scarcely know how we all lived until we got the answer back again, and even when it did come, not one of us liked the task of opening it. No, I don't mean to say that we wasted time in deciding who would do so, but certainly we all dreaded what the slip of paper might contain. It was Father who broke the envelope and first saw the news it brought.

"God be thanked it is ail right," he said. Le Merchant only sends one word— Well.' What a relief! Nancy, thank Heaven your sight was at fault for once."

I thanked Heaven too—we all did; and my people mercifully forbore to tease me about my mistaken vision, and so the autumn weather went on and every day brought us nearer and nearer to our move to the fair shores of the Mediterranean. And then when three weeks had gone by there came another letter from Tom which put the whole matter in a different light. I do not mean that Tom had not written between this letter and that one which had caused my vision, for we had had a letter the very week previously. But this letter was in answer to the telegram.

"I perceive," Tom began, "that Nancy has been at it again. When I tried, and unsuccessfully, to keep a certain incident from you, I had forgotten that time and distance make no difference to Nancy. As a matter of fact, something *has* happened to me, something very unpleasant. I tried to keep it from you, as I did not want any of you to imagine that my life is cast among dangers, and that I was to be worried about continually. I dare say you all know pretty well the truth of what befel me about the time I wrote the last but one. But in case Nancy's sight has not been very complete, I will give you the details. I went to bed one night as usual, leaving my dog—one I doubt if I ever mentioned to you, a big brown fellow standing nearly three feet at the shoulder—loose in my room. I woke up with a sharp stinging pain in my neck and to hear the most awful sounds of growling, struggling and snarling mingled with the most appalling yells and shrieks that it has ever been my lot to listen to. I thought at first that I had been bitten by a snake, though I have never seen so much as the tail of a snake since I landed in India. Some of our servants—I think I told you that there are four of us living together here—came running in bringing in lights. I then saw that Roger, that's the dog's name, had got a native down on the floor and was worrying him fiercely. None of the servants dared interfere and I felt so queer that I could scarcely stand upright. As the lights fell upon me I saw that I was streaming with blood, which was running from a wound in my neck all down my blue cotton pyjamas. I heard my bearer tell one of the others to fetch the doctor, who is one of the four living in this bungalow, and then my head began to swim round and round and I was only conscious that my bearer was holding me up and that another was holding a glass to my lips. And all the time the horrid growling and snarling went on, while the yells got fainter and more choked every minute. I don't know what the doctor did, but by and by I came to myself a bit, and then the chap on the floor was quite quiet and Soger was worrying him and playing with him like a cat plays with a rat.

" 'Who's that?' I asked.

" 'Sahib, we don't know,' my bearer answered. 'We dare not go near the dog. He has tasted blood, and is as savage as a tiger.'

" 'Pooh! the dog's all right. If the beggar had left me alone, he would never have touched him. Here, Roger, old chap, what's up?'

"As I expected, the dog, who is a splendid fellow and perfectly devoted to me, turned his head at the sound of my voice. He thumped his great tail on the floor and then set to work and Worried the man afresh. One of the servants picked up the knife which was still wet with my blood. And then Tennent, that's the doctor, picked up a towel which was lying on the floor a little way off and exclaimed in a sharp tone—'By Jove, this is saturated with chloroform—I smelt it before I got into the room. I believe it's been used to still the dog. Reynard, just see if you can get Roger away, will you? We can't have this mangling going on any longer.'

"Tennent had roughly bound up my neck with a couple of towels, and with his help I got hold of Roger and with a little coaxing I persuaded him to come away and to let the servants carry the body into the adjoining room—for the chap was as dead as a doornail, a sight such as I never want to see again. Tennent just touched the dog's head—'Yes, as I thought, that towel has been used to quiet him, and the fellow was in too great a hurry; he should have waited till the chloroform had had time to do its work effectually. Well, old chap,' he ended, 'you've been a good friend to old Roger, who belonged to a regular brute before you, who used to knock him about for the mere pleasure of seeing him suffer and hearing him howl. But, by Jove, he has repaid his debt with interest. If it hadn't been for him, you'd have been as dead as a herring by this time.'

"And that," the letter went on, "is just about the truth. And the queerest part of it all is that we can't get any clue to the mystery. Why this native chap should have picked me out of all others is incomprehensible. I have no valuables, and if I had it would have been easy enough to make away with them without murdering me over it. I can have made no enemies, for I haven't dismissed a single servant since I came out and am thoroughly satisfied with everybody that I have. I've been very careful—bearing in mind what young asses fellows are who first come out here and that there has been disaffection in the district—not to tread on anyone's corns, and in fact, I feel that I really have not deserved this sort of reward.

"Of course the chap was dead when we got him away from Roger, which saved the trouble and expense of a trial and a hanging, which would have been the inevitable result if Roger had spared him. And I have been quite the hero of Sialkote, which is very embarrassing to a modest mind like mine.

"The only trace of a clue that we found was a paper which was discovered in the man's turban. This is evidently a sort of letter written in cypher, and with the permission of the Colonel I am sending it for Nancy to see. It was indeed by his suggestion, as he thinks that as she found out all about Warrender's diamond star and has evidently got some inkling of this affair, she might be able to trace out this particular piece of villainy. Here in this uncertain land it is most essential that no stone should be left unturned which will help to expose underhand work like this. I must not forget to tell you that I was really very ill for several weeks after that night. I managed to scrawl a few lines, as I did not wish you to be uneasy, and I remembered that two mails had gone by without my writing. I suffered a great deal of pain and a good deal from fever, and I believe both Tennent and Bob Warrender were desperately anxious about me for a couple of weeks. However I am all right now, though a bit pulled down. Old Roger is quite a celebrity and has parties given for him. Think of it. He carries his honours very meekly and sets a fine example to many human persons I know."

Nobody spoke for a moment—then Eve said, "Here is the mysterious paper, Nancy."

CHAPTER X.
THE MYSTERIOUS PAPER.

It is as hard for the good to suspect evil as it is for the bad to suspect good. —CICERO.

And because right is right, to follow right were wisdom in the scorn of consequence. —ŒNONE.

I SUPPOSE with many people the first instinct on hearing such a ghastly story as we had just received from my brother Tom, would have been to say, "Ah, ah, I told you so." But I had no such inclination. You see, we were all thoroughly filled with horror and consternation, and no thought of self came to us. And only too gladly would I have hailed the certain information that my strange power had been at fault; for this story of Tom's proved surely that my gift was in truth a terribly reliable one, and that in future what visions I might see would be real, would be true. Indeed I would much rather have had the comfort of holding this power somewhat in uncertainty.

When my sister Eve held out the mysterious paper to me I half hesitated to take it. I do not think that I ever had such intense repugnance to inquire into the dim recesses of mystery in all my life before. At last, however, I did take it, though my nervous fingers closed over it almost as if they were afraid that it might burn them.

For a moment there was profound silence, as the others sat watching me with breathless interest. Then the scene gradually faded away and another scene came in its place.

"Do you see anything?" I heard my mother ask.

"I see a room that I have seen before," I replied, "it is a rather bare room with a soldier's belongings thrown about; it is the same room that I saw once—I cannot remember where. Yet I have seen it—I've seen it—it is Mr. Warrender's room in

Danford Barracks. Yes, it is the same room—there is nobody in it."

"Try again," said the Colonel, eagerly. "Remember how much is hanging upon it."

"Yes, try—-for dear old Tom's sake," put in Eve. Eve adored Tom.

"Don't talk to me—you disturb me," I said, impatiently. "There is something, but I can't get hold of it. Give me time to breathe."

They stayed as quiet as mice for a little time, and I held the paper tightly between my hands and tried to fix my mind on the influence which had dictated it. Again and again I went back to the room in Danford Barracks, and at last I became conscious that my mind was travelling elsewhere. Slowly, very slowly, a new scene spread itself out before my mental vision—a scene which was wholly new and strange to me, I saw it quite plainly, as plainly as if it had been drawn in a picture.

"I see a very large room with a pointed roof—it is lighted by lamps hanging, by long chains, from the ceiling, or rather the rafters. A man is sitting in a chair by the table; it is a large easy chair, and I can only see the back of his head. It is a dark head, but not native. The town is called Burwarra—Burwarra, or some such name. And the house is—is—oh, what is it? Such a queer name—Tamil, or something like that. Nothing is very clear, except the figure of the man who is sitting with his back to me. He is reading—and now a native servant comes in—he goes near to the table and says something to the man—and the man answers with a nod and a wave of his hand. The native servant is going out—and now he comes back, followed by another native—ah—h, it's the man that stabbed Tom, the man I saw in Tom's room."

I began to feel very sick and faint, but the others begged me not to give way, but to follow the scene to the end, and so I made a great effort and shook myself together again that I might see what was to come Very soon my mind seemed to clear and the whole scene came back to me. "I see them talking together, they are quite near together, but not in an intimate way, for the native cringes the whole time. The man with the brown hair seems to be laying down the law very emphatically and the native bows and cringes and spreads out his hand in a deprecating way, as if to express that the other has but to command for him to obey. Money passes between them and then the man shows the native a sheet of paper and seems to be explaining something to him. At first the native seems to be puzzled, but now he smiles and nods a great many times as if to show that he understands the meaning of the other. Now the native is taking leave, he bows, and puts the palms of his hands together and bows again, then goes back a step or two and bows again. At last he has got himself out of the room and the man is alone."

"Cannot you describe the man?" the Colonel asked.

"No, he has his back turned towards me and has never once looked round. I feel that I should know him if he were to look round. He is familiar to me, and yet I feel that I have never seen him before. He is thinking, thinking deeply. Now he leans his head upon his hand, and although I cannot see his face yet his heart seems to be full of bitterness."

At this point the whole room faded out into a dense white mist and I fancy I slipped off into a semi-unconsciousness; presently, however, it cleared away and a new picture came in its stead. "I see a different place, not a room this time, but a sort of garden. There is a small grove of trees and a doorway, it looks like the doorway into a very small house of only one story. I see the same man, the native who stabbed Tom, he has a paper in his hand and he reads it by the fading light. It grows dark all in a minute, but the native stays there without moving, as if he were thinking of something. I can still see him though it is so dark, for the light from the small house streams through the doorway, and casts a glow over his white clothed figure. Presently he takes a packet from his waistband, it is wrapped in soft paper, and now he opens it. Money—yes, it is money, all in silver, there are a great many silver pieces, like half-crowns, he counts them over and over and looks like a wolf. And then he draws out his knife—oh, it is the same knife that he stabbed Tom with, it makes me sick, I cannot see any more, it is all gone."

I came back to the pleasant room at the Warren with a great shuddering sigh— "Oh, don't ask me to try again!" I cried. "I am done for to-day."

Mother went and fetched me a glass of strong old port and made me drink it before any of them spoke a word to me. I was completely exhausted by my efforts and, after all, I had found out nothing, or what seemed like nothing. However, the Colonel wrote out to Tom and told him what I had seen, and then we had nothing to do but to await the mail which would bring his reply.

In due time that came, and after telling us that he was really quite himself again, Tom told us all that had transpired after the receipt of Father's letter.

"The odd thing is," he wrote, "that Nancy seems to be always right even when she thinks she isn't. It turns out now that the beggar who tried to do for me, and very nearly did too, is a native of Burwarra and came here for the amiable purpose of cooking my goose, straight from there. Burwarra is a rather small station about thirty miles from here, and Tamil is the name of that part of the place where a few good bungalows are situate. We thoroughly investigated—at least the police did—the whole of the Tamil and at last discovered the very bungalow which Nancy describes. It is the only one lighted by lamps suspended by hanging chains. As far as we can make out, the only person answering to the description Nancy gives was a Mr. George Smith, who stayed at this bungalow for a few weeks and gave out that he was travelling in India for pleasure, and not feeling very well, he wished to take a house to himself for a little while, in order to get more quiet than he could in an hotel. Seems to me," Tom added, "that Mr. George Smith meant to ensure me a good spell of peace and quiet, a spell of peace and quiet for which I have no particular fancy just at present. However," he wound up, "it amounts to this, that be that as it may, the beggar who was to do the deed got served out badly enough, and Mr. George Smith isn't likely to try that sort of thing on again with me. If he does he will find me ready for him. I sleep with a revolver under my pillow and I have got another big dog, so that any chance of settling me is very remote. Don't worry about me, dear Mother, and tell the others that I shall turn up again like the proverbial bad shilling."

So we were obliged to let the affair rest and, to tell the truth, I was very thankful to do so. Of course, I could not have refused to do anything which would in any way protect my brother, but my horror of seeing that which would eventually bring some poor wretch to the gallows was very great. I felt as if I never should have got over it, if such a responsibility had come into my life.

Soon after this I was introduced into such society as there was to be introduced to. Mother gave a dance and then Madge gave another, and several friends who had daughters of about my age, did the same, so that we really had quite an unusually gay winter. I was now turned eighteen, a tall slip of a girl, not exactly good-looking, but certainly not ugly. I danced to perfection and everyone said that I had a knack of wearing my clothes well, which is, to a girl, of course a very great advantage; This was the first winter since I was ten years old that we had not spent on the Riviera, and it was with some misgivings that Mother consented to our trying whether I could stand a winter in England, As a matter of fact I was wonderfully well, and I enjoyed the frost and snow immensely. Of course, I was looked after very closely, and old Nurse, who was still with us, followed me round with all kinds of precautions, which I looked upon as both silly and faddy.

About this time, Madge went and had a baby. She and Geoffrey had been married just over seven years, and really they had got on splendidly and had never so much as hinted that babies entered into their scheme of happiness at all. And then this little squalling youngster made his appearance, and everything at Dagenham was changed, and neither the house nor its master and mistress ever were the same again. I really did think that it was weak of Madge, and—in a good moment be it spoken—it was the very horridest baby I had ever seen. I wouldn't have taken it in my arms for all the world, for it squalled and fought and swore at everyone who came near it—yes, swore, quite plainly, though it could not speak, a single word in any ordinary language.

And the fuss that Madge made about that nasty little thing was really foolish. She passed her whole time spooning over it and talking gibberish to it, till it got so pampered that it scarcely knew itself.

And nine days out of ten that baby stopped every plan that its fond and foolish parents had made. If Mother gave a dinner-party, it was a thousand chances to one that a little note would come down, "Darling Mother,—My precious isn't very well, so I am afraid you must excuse me to-night. Geoffrey will come. I hope it won't upset your table."

It always did upset our table, which held fourteen comfortably. And of course it is very difficult to get somebody just at the last moment, because whoever you ask to fill a gap, and no matter how intimately you may know them, they always think that you might have asked them with the first lot. So at last Mother made a rule of never asking more than twelve when she asked Madge and Geoffrey, and that plan certainly worked much better.

I asked Madge one day—when she had thrown Mother over the previous evening and we had not been able to get a fourteenth, which ended in my not coming down to dinner although I had especially wanted to do so—what had been the matter with the baby?

"Oh, poor darling, he was so ill," Madge cried, with an air as if the child had

had convulsions at least—"a great horrid rash came out on his dear little neck, and his mother wouldn't leave him, would she?" and then she poured out such a flood of gibberish at that blob-nosed infant that I, remembering my spoiled dinner-party the previous evening, could cheerfully have shaken her.

"But don't all babies have spots sometimes?" I asked. "Was nurse at all frightened about it?"

"Oh, nurse was quite hard hearted, as I told her," my sister replied. "She wouldn't have it that it ailed anything, but Mother knew what was worrying it, didn't she, ducksie?"

I nearly died of sheer disgust. "Well, look here, Madge, I am going to say something very straight to you, I'm sure I hope you won't be offended, because that is not my intention, I can assure you. But I do wish when you make up your mind at the last moment that you are going to throw Mother's dinner over, that you would make up your mind on another point as well and make Geoffrey stay at home with you. You know as well as I do that our table holds fourteen, and that our number is fourteen, and when you don't come and Geoffrey does, it makes thirteen, which is a very unlucky number. Last night I had to stay away from dinner, and all because you chose to fancy that wonderful baby ailed something. What's the good of having a first-class nurse if you can't stir away for a couple of hours? You could have gone home as soon as dinner was over if you were uneasy, and somebody could have come down every half hour to let you know if it was really ill."

But what was the good of talking? Madge was offended, though I hardly like to ask you to believe it. Yes, she was; and she gathered that ridiculous baby away from the contamination of my presence, as if she thought I had the evil eye and that I might bewitch it. Really, I never saw anyone so spoilt as my sister Madge was by that wretched baby. However, after all, my plain speaking did do some good, for she never played us that same trick again, although Mother took the precaution of only asking twelve when they were coming for quite a long time.

And Eve loved the thing. She was always going over to Dagenham, as she put it "to have a real long, lovely day with the boy." Yes, she even called it a boy—***the*** boy—as if it had been quite a beautiful child. More than once, Eve upbraided me for not taking more notice of it. "I don't know how you can be so unkind to Madge's boy, Nancy," she said to me one day.

"I'm not unkind to it—I was never unkind to anything in my life," I replied, indignantly.

"Why, you never take a bit of notice of it!" she exclaimed—"the only child in the family too."

"My dear Eve," I returned, with a laugh, "you make fuss enough about the youngster for a dozen people. Pray, don't expect me to do the same, because I don't think I ever shall."

CHAPTER XI
THAT BABY!

Conquer we shall, but we must first contend. —HERRICK.

From the gay world we'll oft retire To our own family and fire, Where love our hours employs; No noisy neighbour enters here, No intermeddling stranger near, To spoil our heartfelt joys. —COTTON.

MY sister Eve was god-mother to the Dagenham baby, and the baby was called Reginald de Courcy. It was a strange thing, but as time went on, the baby seemed to get more and more peevish and disagreeable instead of improving, as is the habit of most babies. I have known babies which started with the most peevish and cranky dispositions and which, as the necessary periods of teething and wind have gone by, have been transformed into the most smiling and delightful creatures and in due course of time developed into specimens which were used for advertising certain firms existing for the purpose of supplying infants with divers sorts of food. But Reginald de Courcy, although I am sure he was fed upon every kind of food that has ever been invented for infants, did not thrive on any of them. As every day went, so did that baby get crosser and crosser and his parents more and more demented about it—or if not his parents, certainly his mother did.

My mother was very amusing when she got into conversation about the little heir to Dagenham. "Yes, Madge's baby is nine months old now," I heard her say one day to an enquiring caller—"I'm sure I don't know what to think about him. He is quite unlike any baby *I* ever had. I begin to think they try too many foods for him, poor little fellow. You see, my dear Mrs. Farquhar, I always nursed my babies, and although the new-fangled ways say that a child must be artificially fed and that it is much easier to feed so, yet I don't see that the babies of to-day are any gainers by the change. Now, Madge's boy is always grizzling, and Madge is always in a fever about him. I am sure if she were to let the head nurse—who should be a most experienced woman and who can have next to nothing to do, as Madge gives her an under-nurse—if only Madge would let her have a free hand and manage the child by herself I feel that he would have a better chance all round. But Madge is very self-willed about it and thinks that nobody really understands the child but herself. The result is that the nurse does not do her best and the poor child is the one to suffer."

"I was calling on Mrs. Dagenham the other day," Mrs. Farquhar replied, "and she had the little thing brought down for me to see. Do you know it made me quite sad to see it. Such a little weazened creature! I feel sure that there is something very seriously wrong in its management."

"I have said everything that can be said," said Mother, mildly, "I am very sorry for the poor child, but of course, Madge is his mother and must do what she thinks is best for it."

A few weeks after this, I happened to be lunching with Madge at Dagenham, Eve and I, that is to say. She had the boy at the table and fed it with gravy and potatoes, and every now and then with little bits of chicken from her own plate. Now I had never pretended to take any interest in the child; I had always thought it a horrid little creature and believed that its advent was a great error of judgment on the part of its deluded parents. But at the same time I would not have done the child the very smallest harm, poor little thing; no, I pitied it too much for that.

"I didn't know you gave a baby meat, Madge," I remarked.

"I don't give him meat," she replied ever so sharply.

"A scrap like that helps the teeth, Miss Nancy," put in the head nurse, who was standing behind the little heir's high chair.

Well, I did not know anything about the upbringing of babies, so I did not say anything in reply. But a few minutes afterwards, I caught that woman looking at me in such a furtive and sly sort of way that I felt instinctively she was up to no good.

She took the boy away presently, for his afternoon sleep as she said, and we three went into the long, low drawing-room and sat by the fire talking. That is to say, Madge and Eve talked—chiefly about that blessed baby—and I sat by only joining in now and again and with the new and odd sensation that every remark I made was more or less unwelcome to my hostess-sister.

"Did you try that new food?" Eve asked when we had been chatting for half an hour or so.

"Lady Margaret's food?" said Madge. "Well, yes, we did, but it did not do at all. And Nurse said that she was sure it was quite impossible to ensure its being always exactly the same, on account of the cream being richer one day than another, while the least interruption might spoil the whole of the day's portion."

"I suppose it is very troublesome to make," I remarked.

"Oh, yes a dreadful trouble to make," my sister answered.

"Perhaps your treasure of a nurse does not like trouble," I suggested.

After all, there was nothing in the remark which need have made Madge fly out at me as she did. "Really, Nancy," she burst out—"one would think that Hobson wanted to do the boy an injury by the hints you always throw out about her. Of course, as she says, anyone can see that you don't like her; but you are not going to prejudice me against her. I know too well when I have got a valuable servant to take any notice."

"My dear Madge," I said coolly, "I never said a word against Hobson—why should I? It is nothing to me whether your child thrives or not. Lady Margaret brought up all her delicate children on that food, and it *is* a trouble to make. It is a perfectly natural suggestion that the trouble of making prevents the nurse from taking to it for the child. It seems to me that, for the good of your boy, the sooner you get rid of the valuable Hobson the better. She's a bad lot, that woman."

"Oh, Hobson knows you hate her," remarked my sister, with an air of superb disdain.

"I neither hate her nor the reverse—I would be very sorry to do so," I said, feeling a little indignant that my own sister should have lowered herself so far as to listen to any remarks of a servant against one of her own family. "But of Hobson's ***bona fides*** I am more than doubtful. Anyway, common sense must tell you that it cannot be a proper thing for a child to be as your boy is."

"Oh, what do you know about babies?" demanded my sister.

"Nothing at all, except that your baby is not being done by as it ought to be. I should greatly like to enquire into the good Hobson's by-gone history."

"That is quite above reproach," said Madge, who was now really angry—and oh, how she was changed from the Madge that used to be! "However, as I value Hobson more than words can express, and as I believe your suspicions to be wholly unfounded, I will satisfy you on that point. I got her from Lady Marchmont, with whom she lived five years, and from whom I had a most excellent character."

This of course I knew, but as we had been in the south of France when Hobson had been engaged, I did not know the exact details of the transaction. "Did you see Lady Marchmont yourself? "I asked. Somehow, I did not in the least care whether Madge was vexed or not.

"I wrote to her and have the letter which I received in reply yet," said Madge, in a decidedly huffed tone.

She got up as she spoke and opening a drawer in her writing table took out a packet of letters and selecting one therefrom handed it to me. "There it is," she said. "Now you can judge for yourself."

According to Lady Marchmont's letter, Hobson was indeed a treasure, and the writer had evidently been quite sincere in what she had said.

"Lady Marchmont is that fair, pretty young woman whose photographs one sees about in the shop windows, isn't she? "I asked.

"Yes, she is fair and very pretty," Madge replied.

"Well, Madge, this letter gives me the impression of a stout woman, a good deal older than your Hobson. Your Hobson is dark and thin—Lady Marchmont's Hobson, unless I am very much mistaken, was fairish and decidedly stout, a very good-tempered person and passionately fond of children. I am afraid you have been taken in, my dear, very much afraid."

Really, I never saw Madge in such a boiling rage in all my life. Indeed, up to the time of her marriage, I never had seen her in any kind of a rage at all, for Madge had always been the embodiment of light and sweetness. Now, however, she was just boiling over and she could scarcely contain herself for anger. "Nancy, you let your tongue run away with your wit," she said at last, in a shaking voice. "If Geoffrey hears of this he will be very angry."

"No, no! Geoffrey does not like Hobson any better than I do," I put in, calmly.

The anger all died out of my sister's face. "How do you know that?" she asked, and she looked positively frightened.

"Madge, dear, I've made you very angry," I said, gently. "But, believe me, there is something wrong about Hobson, and your child is paying the penalty, whatever it is. That woman is not the woman whom Lady Marchmont recommended to you, and as for what you say about my hating her, why, it is sheer foolishness. You know perfectly well that I could have no reason for anything of the sort. I daresay she hates me like poison—she is so afraid of my finding her out."

"Finding her out!" repeated Madge.

"Yes, impostors are always afraid of clairvoyantes—it is instinct with them, nothing more."

"I hear her—she is bringing the boy," said Madge, hurriedly. And the next moment, Hobson, carrying the child, entered the room.

I sat watching her pretty closely and not saying much. I noticed that she carefully avoided looking at me, and that she kept as near to Madge as she could. "You can leave Master Reggie here, Nurse," said my sister. "Come for him when you have had your tea."

"Hadn't I better take him, Ma'am?" the woman asked, anxiously. "He will be a great trouble to you; and he does seem so cross and fretful this afternoon. I can't make out why it is. Yesterday he was as bright as a button."

I looked at her, but I could not catch her eye. "No, I will ring if I want you," said Madge, with what seemed like admirable firmness. "And by the bye, Hobson, did you make me out that list of things that are wanted for the nursery?"

"Here, Ma'am," Hobson replied, handing a paper to Madge.

As soon as she was gone out of the room, I put out my hand and took the paper from her grasp. "Let me have it for a minute," I said, in answer to her surprised look.

She yielded to my insistent tone and for a moment none of us moved or spoke. "I see a woman pouring something into a child's feeding-bottle—it is Hobson—stay still, don't interrupt me—she has put a little more sugar into it, and now she is tasting it. Then she takes something from her pocket and puts the feeding-bottle down on the table. It is a little bottle—a blue bottle— and she drops some of the contents into the food—one—one—two—three—four drops. I can't see the label on the blue bottle—stay—no, she has put it back into her pocket."

CHAPTER XII.
THE BLUE BOTTLE.

An evil conscience is always fearful and unquiet. —THOMAS A KEMPIS.

By a divine instinct men's minds mistrust Ensuing dangers; as by proof, we see The waters swell before a boisterous storm. *—**King Richard III.***

POOR Madge! I shall never forget her face when she discovered that the admirable Hobson had been tampering with her precious baby's food.

"Stay a minute," she said, in a very excited tone. "I still have Hobson's first letter to me, that in which she applied to me for a situation. Just wait a minute, Nancy, till I find it."

She went back to the writing-table and began to seareh for the letter with eager and trembling fingers. "Take your time," I recommended. "I am in no hurry."

Madge turned round upon me. "Nancy!" she exclaimed, quite in a passion, "how can you be so cold-blooded! Don't you realise that my only child's life is hanging in the balance—that our all is at stake—that I cannot be calm; while as for taking what you call my time is simply impossible?"

"My dear Madge, if you let yourself get into a flurry, you are simply undone—undone. If you really love that little chap as you profess you will force yourself to keep cool and collected, so as to unmask that wretch upstairs and to leave her no loop-hole of escape. You must not forget that you have to deal with a determined and artful woman and that, even at your best, she will probably prove more than a match for you. Don't waste time abusing me or thinking that I don't set enough store by the youngster, but give your whole thought to showing up this woman in her true colours. Let me help you find it."

Madge, however, managed to find it by herself and turned from the writing-table quite flushed and triumphant, as eager now that I should discover the worst of Hobson, as before she had been anxious that I should think her perfect. She handed me the letter, which I took and read carefully. It was the usual kind of letter that you receive in such circumstances, not very well written, nor yet very well expressed, yet speaking confidently of her capabilities and of the certainty of receiving a good reference. It was some little time before I gathered anything from it but its ordinary contents. Then Madge's pretty drawing-room seemed to fade away and another room to come in its place. "It is awfully queer, Madge," I said, "but the only impression I seem to have is of Mr. Warrender's room in Danford Barracks. I can't understand it. I had exactly the same impression when Tom sent that paper home from India."

"But Hobson could not be in any way connected with Mr. Warrender or his rooms," said Madge, looking as no doubt she felt, very much puzzled. "Do try again."

I held the letter between my two hands once more, but that room came back to me with persistent pertinacity. "I'm sure she is connected in some way with that room," I said—then shut my eyes and tried hard to disconnect myself from that particular influence.

I succeeded better than I had dared to hope for, and presently another scene began to form itself on my mental vision. "Oh, now we are getting nearer," I said. "Yes, I see Hobson quite plainly—she is sitting in a very pretty room near to a window. She is reading a letter, a very long and closely-written letter, on flimsy paper. It doesn't look like Hobson a bit, for she has a smart tea-gown on, a fine pink silk affair, and it has a great deal of lace about the shoulders, and a diamond brooch glitters at her throat. As well as I can make out, it is a name—it looks like John. No, it is not John. . . . It is Joan, I believe. . . . Yes, it is Joan."

"Hobson's name is Matilda," remarked my sister, in an undertone.

"Or she says it is," returned Eve, in the same low voice.

I did not take any notice of either remark. I wanted to keep my mind firmly fixed on the picture which was before me and this kind of sight is very hard to hold, for it is gone almost before one knows it is there, and even a breath of unsympathetic disbelief is often enough to drive away the power for that day.

"She is reading the letter again, reading it very carefully as if she does not like its contents. Now she has turned to a side table and takes a newspaper from a heap lying there, and she turns it over and over as if she is searching for something. Now she has found it and she reads it carefully several times; then sits thinking deeply. She is resting her head on her hand and her thoughts are far from pleasant ones, but she gives her head a decided toss as if she has fully made up her mind about something. Now she gets up and goes to a small cabinet of carved dark wood, she unlocks it and takes out a bottle which she looks at for a moment. She puts it down on the table and reaches for another bottle in the cabinet. That is a blue one, such a one as she has in her pocket now. She goes across the room and pours out the contents into a large plant pot in which an aspidestria is growing. Then she goes to the buffet and fills the blue bottle with water, rinses it out and empties that again into the aspidestria pot. Then she puts the blue empty bottle and the bottle with the white, clear liquid in it, into the cabinet again and she has locked the door. Now she walks to the window and stands looking out into the street, then with a gesture of impatience she sits down at the table and begins to write a letter . . Ah, she is fading away—I can see nothing more. At least not about Hobson—for Warrender's room has come back again. Madge," I broke off with a gasp for breath—"I can do no more."

By this time I was thoroughly played out, and felt almost hysterical. My sister, on the contrary, seemed to have gathered strength and calmness as my nerve became exhausted. She told Eve to ring the bell, with an expression which made me think of a tigress robbed of its cubs—"Bring some brandy and soda at once, please," she said. Then when the man returned with it she ordered him to mix a glass for me and stood over me while I drank it. "Tell Hobson to come here," was her further command.

In a few minutes Hobson came, with a smile on her face and words of affection for the boy who was sitting perfectly contented and happy on Eve's lap. "No, I don't want you to take Master Reginald yet," said Madge in a dangerously quiet voice. "I am going to ask you to do something rather strange, Hobson, but I shall expect you to do it whether it pleases you or not. What have you in your pocket?"

The woman gave a jump—"Nothing out of the ordinary, Ma'am," she protested.

"Then you will have no objection to turn out its contents," said my sister, coldly.

Practically Hobson had no choice but to comply, but she did so with a very bad grace. Slowly she began to take the things out of her pocket, a handkerchief, a pair of small scissors in a sheath, a thimble, an indiarubber ring of the child's and a small purse with a gilt initial on one side of it. "That is not all," said my sister, in a tone of ice.

"That is all, Ma'am," replied Hobson, defiantly.

"I want to see that bottle in your pocket," said Madge, standing close up her and looking straight into her eyes. "Come, Hobson, it is no use trying to get out of this. I know you have a bottle in your pocket, and I mean to see it. Give it to me this moment."

The woman was like a bird fascinated by a snake, and she gave up the bottle without a word. Madge handed it to me. "A blue bottle, you see," she said, significantly.

Then the fury of the woman burst forth. "I have you to thank for this," she cried, passionately, to me. "I've always known you've been against me. I suppose you've been spying after me, making a mountain out of a molehill."

"Hobson !" said my sister in a tone of rebuke and command which accorded most strangely with her belief in Hobson, which I had only just, after much difficulty, dispelled.

She handed the bottle to me, and I took it to the light and examined it carefully. It was a blue fluted bottle, such as is ordinarily used to contain poisons, and on the label was the word "Laudanum," with the address of a London chemist printed below.

"You have been giving my child laudanum!" thundered my sister, in an awful voice.

"Never!" replied Hobson, in a voice of equal firmness.

At this point I took out the cork that I might smell the stuff in the bottle, indeed I emptied a few drops into my glass, just as Hobson went on speaking, in a fierce, grating tone. "Would any woman in her senses give a baby like that laudanum?" she demanded, furiously. "I had the toothache and I did what I always do, I put a few drops on a bit of cotton wool and laid it inside my mounth—there's nothing out of the way in that."

"But this is not laudanum, and you know it," I put in. "And you did drop some of this into the child's bottle—you know it. Four drops. You are slowly poisoning the child, Joan Manning."

The effect of my sudden flash of comprehension upon Hobson was simply electrical. Her face faded to a grey greenish tint, and a sort of spasm convulsed her for a minute or two. In all my life I had never seen any woman so beset with terror; her knees seemed to knock together and her hands shook like aspens. She looked round as if trying to escape.

"The police are not after you yet," I said, significantly. "You will be wanted by and by, and it will be perfectly useless trying to evade justice. A power more cunning and terrible than a bloodhound is on your track, Joan Manning, a power which you cannot fight against, struggle and dodge as you will."

For a moment I thought she was going to break down and make a full confession; but I was mistaken, for she made a sudden rush at me and knocked the little blue bottle out of my hand. "At all events you shall not have anything to show for what you say," she cried, and the next minute Madge had rung the bell, and Eve was standing between her and the door.

It was all over and done in a moment or what seemed so. A couple of men-servants took charge of Hobson, while a third went to fetch a policeman—a village policeman, who declined to interfere without a magistrate's warrant.

Well, you know what an ordinary village policeman is, and this one happened to have once got into trouble for acting on his own responsibility, instead of waiting for a warrant. It was no use. Madge stormed and raved, and the men-servants made remarks which were perfect specimens of caustic wit, but the village guardian of the peace was inflexible and not an inch would he budge. So while we were waiting in a state of paralysis, Matilda, *alias* Joan Manning, put most of her things together and betook herself away.

And what a commotion it was which followed! Geoffrey Dagenham came home in time for dinner and heard the whole story almost before he had crossed the threshold, and when he gathered how that village policeman had been crass idiot enough to let a murderous woman escape on a mere technicality, his rage and fury really were beyond control.

However, it was no use to rage and storm. Raging and storming do not undo what has been done, and Joan Manning was gone—had indeed got several hours' start of us all. The lady had, however, reckoned somewhat without her host, when she had, as she thought, so cleverly knocked the little blue bottle out of my hand. For I had still got possession of the few drops which I had poured into my glass, more from curiosity than anything else. Geoffrey sent down for the doctor, who came and smelt it, then tasted it, looking very wise and as if he knew a great deal about it, when in truth he was profoundly ignorant of the whole matter.

"I had better keep the broken pieces of the bottle," said Geoffrey," and put this," touching the glass, "into a sound bottle and cork it up tight. To-morrow I will take it up to London and get it analysed. I shall follow the affair up to the extremest end."

It is scarcely necessary in the interests of this story to follow this extraordinary incident so far as that. It is enough to say that my sister apologised to me very prettily that night for what she had said in the earlier part of the afternoon, and that Geoffrey set the whole machinery of the law at work, and with such good effect that Joan Manning was soon in the hands of the police, and that such custody resulted in her receiving a sentence of two years' hard labour, together with a compliment from the judge on the extreme lightness of her sentence. And as Eve remarked that evening at dinner—"There won't be any more pink silk tea-gowns for Joan Manning until she has had ample time for reflection over the mutability of human hopes and desires."

CHAPTER XIII.
THE RUBY CLARET JUG!

In much wisdom is much pain. —***Ecclesiastes.***

Into the Silent Land, Ah! who shall lead us thither? Clouds in the evening sky more darkly gather, And shattered wrecks lie thickest on the strand. Who lead us with a gentle hand, Thither, O, thither, Into the silent land? —LONGFELLOW.

SIX months had gone by since Joan Manning, ***alias*** Matilda Hobson, had been consigned to durance vile for her attempt to take the life of my sister's little son. By that time the whole neighbourhood was in the secret of my wonderful gift, and any idea we might, as a family, once have had as to keeping it strictly to ourselves, had been dispelled for ever.

I cannot say that, on the whole, I found my existence at all improved by this knowledge becoming general. From the time of Joan Manning's trial I was a marked person. When I went to a party, people used to look at me exactly as if I had the evil eye and might scorch their very souls by so much as glancing at them. Mothers used to tremble if their daughters were left alone with me, and perfect strangers used to come to me with all sorts of the most flimsy excuses to bespeak my good offices to unravel the most extraordinary tangles in their lives.

I believe I had grown up very much prettier than I had promised to be when a girl; so that when I went to dances, which was rather frequently, it used to be very amusing to see young men casting their eyes around in search of partners and then to see them turn to some friend to ask who I was and if they could be introduced to me? The answer was always given in the same sort of way—with a mysterious whisper followed by an expression of much astonishment from the enquirer, I knew so well just what was being said. "I say, old chap, who's that girl? Rather pretty, ain't she? Wish you'd introduce me." And then the answer—"Delighted to, but—don't you know—she's not quite like other girls. Swagger enough and all that, but a bit queer in some ways. Got second sight, or the evil eye, or something—always finding out things about people and splitting about 'em at inconvenient moments. By Jove, if you've ever murdered anybody or stolen a will or anything of that kind, I wouldn't advise you to go in for her, no, I wouldn't, by Jove."

And some of them used to sheer off in a highly uncomfortable way, though whether they had ever murdered anybody or stolen a will or done anything else of that kind, I could not say. And some of them used to boldly go for me and then try to lead me out upon occult matters, of which, by the bye, I was painfully ignorant. I don't know much about such things now, but then I was just as blissfully ignorant as the babe unborn. While as for my indisputable gift of second sight, I really did not know much about that either. When it had possession of me, I felt the effects of it; but of its workings I was profoundly unknowing.

From the very first time that the general knowledge of my gift began to creep out among our acquaintances, the Colonel rigidly set his face against my being made use of in any way for acting as a detective. So when people came, asking if I would find out for them if a friend was true or false to them, or whether such and such a person was straight or not, he always emphatically forbade my interfering in any way with the affairs of others. "But, Colonel Reynard," a gentleman expostulated one day, when my father had forbidden me to try to find out who had stolen certain bonds of his, "do you think that you are right or justified in keeping your daughter's great power as a private matter?"

"Right or wrong, I will not allow her to exert this force for the benefit of strangers," my father replied. "You, sir, are a total stranger to me and, to be frank, I regard this request as a distinct intrusion. You must be perfectly well aware that no young girl can exert such a force without giving out a large share of her vitality. Why should my child give out her vitality for you? What are your bonds to us? Her vitality is something to her, it is her very life. You may get your bonds back, but vitality once exhausted can never be brought back again. Besides that, my daughter is not a professional clairvoyante and never will be. You have as much right to go and ask the Queen to dance a jig for you, as you have to come and ask my daughter, who is an absolute stranger to you, to exert, for your own ends, a power which is a very great responsibility and annoyance to her already."

With that, of course, the gentleman had to be satisfied, as indeed there was no more to be said. He went away somewhat crest-fallen, and the Colonel read me what, for him, was quite a lecture on the evils that would follow if I ever allowed myself to be persuaded to use my power for the benefit of persons to whom it might be convenient.

As a matter of fact, however, for a long time after everything came to light about Joan Manning, or rather after Joan Manning was put out of the way of doing any more mischief of that particular kind, my life flowed on in quite ordinary grooves and I saw nothing out of the common. Indeed, I began to think that my power had completely exhausted itself. But eventually it proved not so, for I was sitting in the garden one day with Mother and Eve, when a sudden vision came to me.

It was the first time in my life that any vision had ever come to me other than by actual contact; invariably, I had had touch of some kind with those whom I saw, some connecting link between my brain and the other brain far away with which I suddenly found myself *en rapport.* This experience was, however, entirely different. As a matter of fact, we had had several visitors and the day being exceedingly oppressive, Mother had ordered some claret to be brought out for the doctor, who came in for a little friendly chat. Poor man, he was very tired, I remember, and the claret was very grateful to him. And when he had revived a little, he turned to me and asked me a question, "How go the visions, Nancy?" he said, in a joking tone.

"All gone, Doctor," I replied. "And I don't believe there are going to be any more visions. I don't really."

"My dear child," said he, growing quite grave, "I am exceedingly glad to hear it. I am quite sure that they are very, very bad for you because they are bound to exhaust you tremendously. Probably as you grow stronger, you will outgrow the tendency altogether. Indeed, I don't believe, if you had been a really robust child, that you would ever have known anything about such things at all."

Alas, alas, within an hour of that kindly comment my power exercised itself once more, and one of the saddest visions that I had ever seen came to me. We had had several callers since the dear old doctor had left, and we three were sitting under the trees chatting idly. Mother had a bit of work in her hands and Eve was very busy tracing an embroidery pattern which she was going to use for something pertaining to Madge's boy. I had a couple of illustrated papers which had just come and was glancing at them in a very perfunctory way, trying in short to do two things at once and not succeeding very well, for the papers got sadly neglected. And presently silence fell upon us. Mother was absorbed in her work, and Eve was bending down over hers. I had been carelessly looking at the pictures when I somehow found myself staring at the claret jug, which was a beautiful thing of ruby Bohemian glass and worth far too much money to be out in a garden where it ran every risk of getting broken. I never knew what made me fix my eyes upon it, but I was startled to find that pictures were forming on the plain ruby surface of the rounded jug, pictures quite as clear to me as if they were painted on a canvas.

As I sat there the pictures seemed to be moving, as it were, growing or developing before my astonished eyes. I uttered an exclamation of surprise and my mother looked up from her work. "What is it, Nancy?" she asked.

"It is the strangest thing I ever knew," I replied; "pictures are coming out of the claret jug—why, it is a mess-table and all the officers are at dinner. I can see Tom and Mr. Warrender as clearly as possible."

"What?" cried Mother and Eve in the same breath.

"Yes, they are siting next to each other and oh, Mother, Tom does look so ill. He keeps resting his head on his hand as if it ached. I am sure he is ill. Now Mr. Warrender is speaking to him, but Tom does not answer. Mr. Warrender touches him on the arm as if to try to attract his attention. Tom never moves. Mr. Warrender turns and looks down the long table and makes a gesture of his head to another officer, a much older man, whose hair is turning grey. He gets up and comes round to Tom's chair and bends over him. Tom just shakes his head but does not raise his face. They all get up and are moving Tom's chair back and several of them have lifted it up bodily and are going to carry him away on it. Ah—it is all fading away into a thick white mist. I think that is all. Mother, I'm sure Tom is ill—Stay, something else is coming! Oh, this is a great bare, gaunt room with several native servants standing about all looking thoroughly scared, and they keep whispering together and shrugging their shoulders and looking at the bed round which all the others are gathered. They have thrown the thin white curtains back and are all evidently helping to do something. Now two or three of them are moving away a little and stand at a little distance; they all look grave and sad, and the older man, who must be the doctor, is feeling Tom's pulse and counting it by his watch. Then he gives him some clear white medicine in a wineglass. He says something to Warrender, who nods his head and looks at Tom again. Tom is fearfully ill, oh, fearfully ill. He looks quite insensible and he is bluish in colour. There is a lamp burning, and the several officers in mess-dress stand on one side of the bed as if they did not know what to do next, and the native servants stand a little way off all huddled together and frightened out of their senses almost. Only the doctor and Mr. Warrender stay quite near to the bed, and then the doctor gets up and says something to the others and they one by one, with a look at Tom, creep out of the room. Then he moves towards the servants and apparently gives them each some directions, for they, too, go oat, leaving only Tom and the other two. Then the doctor puts his hand on Mr. Warrender's shoulder and says something in a very urgent sort of way, but he only shakes his head and does not move. Then the doctor puts his hand under his arm, as if to help him up from the chair, but Mr. Warrender only shakes his head the more vigorously and makes a gesture as if the other may save his words. I think he is asking him to go away and that Mr. Warrender refuses, for the older man shrugs his shoulders and turns out his hands palm uppermost as if there is nothing else that he can say.

"Now he is bending down over Tom again. Oh, Mother, Tom is *very* ill, very very ill! He seems to be shuddering dreadfully, and now two of the natives come back carrying something wrapped in a blanket or woollen rug. The doctor takes it from them and—yes, it is a hot water-bottle and he is putting it to his feet. There is another and yet another in the blanket and he puts them all under the bed-clothes, and then he is giving Tom some more of the medicine, the white, clear medicine out of the same bottle as before. I don't think Tom is quite unconscious, for he is speaking to Mr. Warrender who bends down over him. The doctor pulls him back and holds his head back quite sharply. Mr. Warrender has hold of Tom's hand and the doctor fusses about, doing things. He comes back and takes his pulse again and then his temperature. It is all fading out again—and the white mist comes back, so I can see nothing more."

"Go on looking for something, try, try to see what else," cried Mother, in an agonised tone.

"You *must* see the rest," put in Eve, with desperate anxiety.

The rest! Oh my dear, dear Tom, if only I had not been the one to see what happened next, to see what followed in the terrible afterward.

"Don't talk—something is coming now," I said, for by speaking they distracted me and kept me back from a full realization of what followed. "Yes, it is the same room and the doctor and Mr. Warrender are both there and several other men, one a very tall, fair-haired man about forty years old. There are two servants by the bed, but not quite so near as the others. Mr. Warrender is sitting close by the bed, and now the doctor looks round. I don't think Tom knows anything that is going on. He is lying very much sunk down among the pillows, his head very far back and his eyes half shut. Somebody else is coming in now, a man wearing plain white clothes and a black band round his arm. He holds up his hand as he reaches the threshold and is speaking. All the others bow their heads and the tall fair man makes way for him by the bed. He kneels down and is praying, and the others all kneel down, too, except the natives, who are standing up with their heads bent upon their chests. Mr. Warrender is kneeling too, and he has hidden his face in Tom's pillow—only Tom takes no notice and he lies just the same, with his eyes half shut, deep down among the pillows. I—I—don't think I can go on, Mother." I broke off.

Mother made a sort of a moan. "My boy, my boy, tell me the rest, Nancy, tell me the rest."

The agony in her voice was so great that I shook myself together again and turned my eyes back on the ruby surface on which I had seen mirrored what was happening many thousands of miles away. The surface was blank, but as I gazed, it all came back to me. The group of men were almost unchanged, the one in plain white clothes was still kneeling, though the others had risen, with the exception of Tom's great friend, Mr. Warrender.

As I looked on the scene, there was a general movement which ran through all the watchers by my brother's bed. I saw the doctor put up his hand, and that Warrender's shoulders were heaving, the tall fair man was covering his eyes with his hand—"Mother, ask me no more!" I cried—"We have no Tom now!"

CHAPTER XIV.
AN INDIAN TELEGRAM.

As the smell of the sea cleaves to the sea-plant for long years, so the love of the dead clings to the living. —LYNCH.

Wealth and dominion fade into the mass Of the great sea of human right and 'wrong, When once from our possession they must pass; But love, though misdirected, is among The things that are immortal, and surpass All that frail stuff which will be or which was. —SHELLEY.

THE pictures that I had seen mirrored on the surface of the ruby claret-jug proved, alas, to be too true, true in every small detail. Not that my people or I doubted it for a moment. From the time that I had seen the doctor hold up his hand and the tall fair man (whom we afterwards found was the Colonel of the regiment), cover his eyes with his hand, I knew as well as if I had actually been present in the same room with them that my dear brother had passed from this world to another. Even my mother never seemed to cling to a faint hope that I might have been deceived for once; oh, no, from that moment she mourned her eldest son as one who had been taken away from her and she was inconsolable.

And in an incredibly short time the message came which confirmed my visions; it was cruelly short, as all such messages are, but for us it was more than long enough. We knew all the details but too well! We were making a pretence of eating dinner when it came. The Colonel was just trying to persuade Mother to eat something when old Nurse came trembling in, carrying the orange envelope in her shaking hand. It was not usual for Nurse to show at meal-times, but none of the others liked to bring it in; they all felt instinctively that the old woman who had nursed us all would bear the ill-tidings best. We all knew—Mother gave a sort of shuddering gasp and dear Daddy held out his hand to take the envelope. "Give it me, Nurse, my dear old woman," he said, in a very gentle voice. "You need not try to break it to us. We know what it is."

So Nurse handed the telegram to him and went and stood by Mother, holding her arm round her shoulders as if to shield her against what was coming. Father read the message in silence going on carving—oh, carving did I say? I meant rather blindly hacking at a chicken, as a sightless man might have done. A glance was sufficient to tell me the contents of the paper—"Your son died this morning of cholera.—Le Merchant."

Yes, that was all, not a word more; but alas, it was enough. It was a dreadful time which followed. For many weeks Mother never gave way at all, but went about like a woman of stone, with terrible tearless eyes and restless hands that seemed able to occupy themselves with nothing. Even when the letters came which gave us final details, she never wept or broke down at all. There was one from Colonel Le Merchant to Father, and one from Tom's great friend, Mr. Warrender, to Mother. The former was the shorter of the two but was full of regret and sympathy. Colonel Le Merchant spoke so highly of our dear boy, said that he was such a good and enthusiastic soldier and so honourable and full of tact, and that he was sincerely mourned and regretted by all ranks of the regiment. He added that everything that human power could do had been done, and that the doctor had never left him from the time of his seizure until the time of his death. Also that he had been present himself when the end came.

The other letter was different; it was full of tear blots and mistakes, but it gave us the whole sad story from the beginning of Tom's Bhort illness to the very end—exactly what he had last said, and how the doctor had stayed by him and done everything that could possibly have been done, until it was useless to try to avert the end. "I am afraid, dear, kind Mrs. Reynard," he went on, "that the telegram was an awful shock to you, and yet I feel sure that in some way the event would reveal itself to Miss Nancy, and that you already know all that there is to know—he, dear old fellow, thought so too. 'I don't think I shall weather this, old chap,' he said, after we had got him into his own bed, 'I don't feel like it. If I don't, you'll write home and let my people know everything and tell them I thought of them all to the very end. But I daresay Nancy knows all about it already!' "

Poor Mother, she carried that letter about until it was worn to tatters, and she read and re-read it, though she must have known every word by heart. "That is a dear boy," she said, when she read it the first time. "God keep *his* mother from ever knowing such pain as I feel; but if the like should ever come to him, may there be a heart as faithful as his at hand," and then she stole away in her dreadful voiceless grief leaving us all with quivering lips and overflowing eyes. Poor Mother!

As time went on, we got used to the idea that Tom had really gone; for a long while it seemed to all of us, even to Mother, as if he were still out in India and would come home by and by, the same dear, jolly old Tom whom we had loved and teased and plagued all our lives. For a long time it was a terrible wrench to each one of us who were left at home, when we were brought back to a realization of the truth that Tom was gone—gone for always, that Tom would never come home again, that he was lying in his early grave under an Eastern sky and was now nothing more to us than a dear memory and vague shadowy hope.

Yet time does wonders for us when we lose those who are dear to us; and time did great things for us in this respect. We had never tried to shut him away out of our lives, as so many people do with their dead; for one thing the doctor warned us that for Mother's sake we must avoid all attempt to repress our sorrow, and that the more we talked about Tom, the better chance our mother would have of finding a natural vent for her grief. And so it proved; one day, after some weeks had gone by, Eve found Mother crying over some old belongings of Tom's, and from that hour the clouds were lifted from her brain and she became her ordinary self once more. No, I do not mean to convey that Mother had not been in her right mind up to that time—nothing of the kind. Yet without doubt if the strain of grief which could find no natural outlet had continued the consequences might have been most disastrous to her reason. And to us who loved her, it was terrible to see that awful, voiceless, stunned sorrow; so that we were utterly thankful when the phase passed.

We spent that winter in Italy, not staying in one place but moving about, as our fancy prompted us to do. Nearly six months had gone by since Tom's death. Christmas had come and gone and the New Year was already a few days old. We had been for several weeks in Naples, to which place we had gone because Mother fancied it. And we were beginning to think of working our way homewards by very easy stages, with long rests by the way.

How well I remember the day on which we first met Austin Gray. We had been for a long drive, a sort of pilgrimage to a shrine of beauty, and had been away from the hotel since early morning; and when we got back again, the first thing that we heard was that several fresh visitors had arrived They were not all of one party, an American father and mother with three daughters, a son and several hangers-on, had come from Rome; but this Mr. Gray, who was quite alone, said that he had been spending a few weeks in southern Italy and was last from Sorrento, of which he spoke in terms of the most rapturous praise.

Somehow, we did not take very readily to the American party—not because we were by way of sniffing at Americans, as some English people pretend to do; but this particular set were in no need of new acquaintances and, being so many in themselves, had no special desire to know us any better than just well enough to say good morning at the beginning of the day and good-night at the end of it. But Mr. Gray being English and alone, and we only three (for Eve had gone back to stay with Madge some little time before Christmas, taking the opportunity of travelling home with some friends whom we had met in Rome), it seemed quite natural that he should attach himself to us and that we should make no objection to include him in our little outings, all of which were very quiet and simple, and apparently not much calculated to attract a man who had seen so much and done so much as he seemed to have done.

And yet he was evidently very well satisfied to make the fourth of our party, and for several weeks we went here, there, and everywhere together, and at last it grew to be quite a settled thing that where we went Mr. Gray should go too, and we had long ago given up the formality of asking him or he of suggesting to Mother that if she didn't mind, he would like to join us in such and such an excursion.

My father spotted him for a soldier at once—"I see you've been in the Service too," he said to him, during the very first talk that he had with us.

"Yes, I was some years in the Service," Mr. Gray replied. "But I got so tired of it and there seemed to be no prospect, either of promotion or of active service, that I felt as if I were just wasting my time when I might be occupying it to better advantage. Since I left the Army, I have done some big shooting and I rather fancy that I shall try a turn of exploring next year."

"Do you?" said my father. "Well, I always say let those who like that kind of work go in for it. I never had the least inclination for anything of the sort."

Mr. Gray glanced at my mother and then at me—"Ah, but if you were quite alone in the world, as I am, you would understand the fascination of doing something a bit out of the common. Not but what I would stand in your shoes to-morrow if I could."

"Similar shoes are very easy to find," said the Colonel, with a gay laugh—"if you really want to find them. But you are quite right, a wife and a home of your own do make you less enterprising."

Then Mr. Gray began to talk to me. He talked well and easily, touching on many subjects and speaking with a certain amount of cultivation on every topic which cropped up in our conversation. "What regiment were you in?" I asked him, when we had been chatting for half an hour or so.

"In the Blankshire," he replied.

"Oh, were you really?" I exclaimed. "That was Mr. Caspar Barry's regiment."

"Caspar Barry—why, do you know him?" our new friend cried. "Why, I was three years with Caspar Barry. What a dear old fellow he was!"

"Yes, he was; we all liked him immensely—especially Father and I." I really added this as an after-thought, for as a matter of fact, Caspar Barry was once a great flame of Eve's and had, so to speak, shaken the dust of our domicile off his feet about two years before, and Eve had been hard-hearted enough to laugh and to declare with an air of fine scorn, that Caspar Barry had not really cared a fig for her, but had been solely moved to admiration of her by the fact that she was the only girl he had ever met who had not promptly fallen down and worshipped him.

We used to wonder, Mother and I, how it was that Eve, who was so pretty and bright and clever, should be so very hard to please in the matter of her admirers, but I am bound to say that Eve was always entirely consistent and sent them all to the right-about in double-quick time. "Time enough, time enough," she would cry, when Mother ventured to put in a word for some discarded adorer. "I am very well as I am. I don't want to leave home yet awhile; by and by, I will see what I can do to oblige you."

"I am so afraid when Eve does take a fancy to anyone," Mother sighed one day to me, after just such an off-hand speech from my sister, "that she will have it badly—and that so often means trouble, especially for a woman. I really do wish that she had been more like Madge; there's safety in numbers."

"And Madge did have numbers," I reminded her, laughing.

Well, it is no use wasting time in wishing that people, over whom one has absolutely no control, were different to what they are. For myself I never troubled about the matter. If Eve, who was five years older than I was, chose to keep all the men she knew at a distance, why, it was her business, not mine. But that was how Caspar Barry came into the story.

"I suppose you don't know where he is now?" I remarked when we had further discussed some of Caspar Barry's charming qualities.

"The last time I saw him he was just off to the Rockies for an indefinite stay," he replied.

"Oh, then he really did go to the Rockies; he said he would, but people do change their minds so. One never knows whether they really mean what they say."

"Oh, yes, he really did go—at least, to the best of my belief," Mr. Gray said.

I told Eve the news when I next wrote to her; but she did not seem to be at all contrite for having driven a poor young man away from his native land with a sore, sore heart, like a wounded animal that only wants to get somewhere out of sight of every eye. Girls are very hard of heart, and Eve was especially so. She wound up her letter with a little dig at me on the score of our new friend.

"I feel, dear old Nancy," she said, when she had disposed of poor Caspar Barry, "that you are going to fall in love with this new friend, Mr. Gray. Your letter is quite full of him, and poor old Caspar only acquires a certain degree of importance in your eyes, because he was in the same regiment with this Austin Gray. It's a pretty name and you say its owner is good-looking as well. It is evident to me that he must be simply perfection, for you seem to have found out nothing about him. Does he know you yet? I mean does he know about your wonderful gift? If not, I should not dream of telling him a single word about it. Dear me, I wonder did you know how quite full of him your letter is? I can hardly imagine you in love, Nancy; you have always been such a cold little thing towards men. By the bye, did it ever strike you how utterly unlike you and I are to Madge, who was a regular flirt and no mistake about it, and who really and truly, as I always tell her, did not in the least deserve to end by getting such a delightful husband as dear old Geoffrey?"

I sat thinking deeply when I had read my sister's letter through, turning over in my mind all that she had said about our new friend. Was I falling in love with him? Was he falling in love with me? I did not know, I could not tell; only I did know this, that I never had any feeling that there was anything to find out about him, never, never once.

CHAPTER XV.
AUSTIN GRAY.

A thousand pleasant hopes That fill your heart with happiness. —*The Spanuh Student.*

Earth's stablest things are shadows, And, in the life to come, Haply some chance-saved trifle May tell of this old home; As now sometimes we seem to find In a dark crevice of the mind, Some relic, which, long pondered o'er, Hints faintly at a life before. —JAMES RUSSELL LOWELL.

WHEN six weeks had gone by we were still lingering on at Naples. The place suited us perfectly, and Mother seemed better and brighter than she had done at any time since our dear Tom's death. The climate was perfect, we could sit out of doors watching the lovely blue sea rippling under the yet bluer sky, when it made us all shiver to even think of sitting down for a moment in the open at home in England. And we took advantage of the possibility, every one of us, for the hotel had a charming garden with a terrace and we used to sit there for hours together. I well remember one afternoon that my Father had gone down into the town—if the truth be told on the look-out for some queer old plates of which he had heard the previous day and which, from the description given by a young American staying in the hotel, he believed to be of great value. They were in a rather squalid part of the town and he had preferred to go alone. Mother was busy writing to Madge and also to Dick, whose birthday was drawing near and who was steadily making way at the business which he had chosen for his walk in life. She was writing at the window of our sitting-room and I was sitting in the sunshine with a big white umbrella and a book, when Mr. Gray came out of the hotel and joined me. I had seen him before that day, for he always sat near to us at meals, and I quite thought that he had gone curiosity-hunting with the Colonel. I told him so.

"No," he replied, "I gathered that your father did not care about having a companion. He is after some unusually rare prize and wants to have it all to himself. Has he always had this love for curios?"

"Most decidedly not," I returned with a laugh," It is quite a new mania. Ever since we came abroad this time, he has been steadily collecting things, and the strangest part of it is that although it is quite recently that he has taken to it, he seems to know a good thing when he sees it by a sort of intuition. He has picked up some really wonderful bargains; but Eve, my sister, you know, took most of them home with her when she went before Christmas."

"Your sister went home before Christmas," said Mr. Gray, in a wandering kind of tone, as if his thoughts were very far away.

"Yes, she is staying with my married sister at Dagenham, not far from where we live, near Minchester. Do you know that part at all?"

"I have been in Minchester for a day or two," he replied.

"Have you? And do you know anyone there? "I asked.

"Not a soul, not anyone. I went down to look at a place there—no, not for myself, but for a friend. She did not take it—she took a dislike to the place instead."

"That was very unfortunate—for Minchester," I said, laughing again.

"But I mean to go to Minchester again and I mean to like it very much indeed—that is unless someone is very unkind to me and tells me it is no use going there at all." He spoke meaningly and I felt myself growing as red as a peony.

"What do you think?" he asked.

"Oh—well, it would depend on why you wanted to go there," I returned, trying hard to speak in quite an ordinary tone.

For answer he took possession of the big umbrella and held it so as to shield us from observation. "Nancy—I may call you so, may I not?—you know what I mean. If I come to Minchester at all, it will be to see you, and if you send me away, Minchester—and every other place for that matter—will be all black and dreary, just as England and the Atlantic and the Rockies are to poor old Caspar Barry. You won't be hard of heart like your sister, will you? Speak, Nancy."

I did not speak, because I scarcely knew what to say. I felt—what did I feel? In truth, I hardly know. He took possession of my hand and it lay trembling in his grasp, like a bird that scarcely knows whether to struggle or to remain still in the prison in which it has found itself. "Have you nothing to say to me?" he asked reproachfully.

"I don't know—I don't know," I cried, "What am I to say?"

He laughed outright. "Nancy, my dear little girl," he said in a greatly amused voice, "I think that there are very few men who wish to marry who would not prefer to be the first, the very first lover to the girl to whom they wish to be everything. It is very evident to me that you are—that is, that there has never been anyone else in your life, and that I am your very first lover. It is so, is it not?"

"Are you my lover?" I asked, wonderingly.

"I want to be so," he replied promptly. "Whether I am or not depends, of course, on you."

"But you don't seem to be in love with me," I explained. "Are you really, really?"

He dropped the umbrella still lower and caught my hand in his. "I—Nancy, my darling—look at me, don't you think I am in love with you enough? Why, how much in love would you like me to be?"

He caught hold of both of my hands, letting the umbrella take care of itself, which it did by catching against my sleeve—"Nancy—my darling—my love—," and then somehow he drew me close to him and kissed me.

It was the first time that anyone—I mean that any man—had ever kissed me, and I shivered from head to foot as if I had been struck by a blast of cold air.

"Nancy," he cried, "Nancy—have you nothing to say to me? You do love me, you must love me, Nancy."

I drew myself back a little from the clasp of his jealous arms. "Mr. Gray——"

He held me still closer. "Well, Mr. Gray is listening," he said, as I paused and looked at him.

"You are not very reasonable—you have not told me yet that you care for me either," I said.

"Did not my words tell you so? Do I not look as if I loved you? See this," holding out his hand, which was trembling violently—"is not this proof enough for you? What do you expect, how can I satisfy you? Nancy, I believe you are only trying to tease me."

"I am not trying to tease you," I cried, half indignantly. "I never tried to tease anyone in that way in all my life, never. It isn't kind of you to say so, Mr. Gray."

He looked all penitence in a moment. "Darling," he said, taking up the umbrella again and adjusting it anew, "I humbly beg your pardon if I said anything untrue; but here I am, patiently waiting, waiting to hear you say one little word and you persist in not saying it. It is ever so easy. Come, won't you satisfy me?"

"You know I like you," I said, at last.

"Like—like—oh, what's liking?" he repeated in huge disdain. "I want my wife to do more than like me, Nancy. I want my wife to worship me."

"But I don't," I objected.

"But you might at least try—Oh, Nancy, dear little sweetheart, you might try."

He was holding my hands tightly in his own again and looking eagerly into my eyes. I felt like a puzzled and half-frightened child, as if I did not know how to cope with this sudden whirlwind of affection. I drew back a little. "You—you frighten me," I managed to say.

Mr. Gray let go my hand and as it were shook himself together. He sat back, quite away from me and his eyes drooped before mine. I felt all at once that I had been utterly unkind to him. "Don't look like that!" I exclaimed. "I did not mean to hurt you. Did I seem unkind? Forgive me, you know I am not used to this sort of thing."

I held out my hands again and he caught them in his, then bent down and kissed them passionately many times. "Nancy," he said, in a glad, triumphant tone—"Mine, all mine! Tell me once, only once, that you really love me."

But instead of telling him so I sat and stared at him in utter wonder. "Tell me,"

I said—"Where did we ever meet before that evening when you came from Sorrento? I am sure I met you long ago—Where was it?"

CHAPTER XVI.
ENGAGED.

So much in this world depends upon getting what we want. Prosperity is to the human heart like a sunny south wall to a peach. —HOLME LEE.

Take joy home, And make a place in thy great heart for her, And give her time to grow, and cherish her. —JEAN INGELOW.

WHEN I said to Austin that I was sure I had seen him somewhere or other before the evening of his arrival at Naples, from Sorrento, he caught me to him and kissed me a dozen times in that strange, bold, masterful way which was quite his greatest charm. "My dear little girl," he said, holding me closely to him and looking right down into my eyes, "that is the greatest proof that you and I were meant for each other. Do you know I believe, firmly and absolutely, that certain people are always put in the same relation to each other, no matter how many lives they may live, no matter in what ages their separate lives may happen to fall."

"But you don't think we live more than once!" I exclaimed, in utter astonishment.

"Why, of course I do. I believe that every one of us goes on living over and over again until we accomplish the end for which we are meant. Sometimes, according to the way in which we have behaved ourselves here—that is, in the past life, the last life—we get quite near to our affinities; sometimes we—for every one of us go up or down according to our deserts—are stranded far apart from them. How else do you account for our curious feeling that we have met certain people before? How else do you account for the most unlikely people remaining unmarried? How else do you account for some people marrying immeasurably beneath them? Fate, my dear child, fate, nothing else."

"It is a curious creed," I said, reflectively.

"As curious as the second sight," he put in, not looking at me, but right out across the sparkling blue waters.

For a moment I was tempted to tell him-about my strange gift A kind of cold shiver ran through me, and a swift, sudden instinct rose up like a beacon light, saying, "Not yet, not yet; keep your own counsel. Silence is golden." So I let the opportunity pass and said nothing about it at all.

Perhaps it was not very honest of me; but, somehow, I did shrink from disclosing myself to him in that one way. He went on speaking, but, oddly enough, not on the same subject. "Tell me," he said, and he spoke as if we had been discussing the matter before—"Is your sister at all like you?"

"Do you mean Eve, or my married sister, Mrs. Dagenham?" I asked.

"I meant the one you speak of so often," he replied, "the one who went home before Christmas."

"That is Eve. No, she is not at all like me."

"You mean to look at," he said, carelessly. "But I meant in disposition."

"I don't know that she is. She is much more intense than I am. When Eve once takes an idea in her head, wild horses would not drag it out again. We used to call her the bull-dog when we were all little, at least poor dear Tom called her so, and we all took the idea from him."

"And Tom—why do you speak of him like that?"

I felt my eyes fill with tears. "I thought we had told you about him long ago," I cried. "Our dear, dear Tom—he died of cholera last year in India."

He looked all penitence and concern in a minute.

"Forgive me," he said, very softly—then touched my black frock—"and that is why you are wearing this," he said, gently.

"Yes, that is why, and that is really why we are abroad this winter. We would rather have been at home, though we have spent a good many winters abroad; but my mother felt dear Tom's death dreadfully, oh dreadfully, and Father thought there was nothing like a complete change for her. She is wonderfully better, though, you know, nothing will ever quite take the pain of our loss away from any of us."

"And you were all very devoted to him?" he asked.

"Oh, yes, we are all very fond of one another. I think if there was anything to choose among us; that Eve idolised Tom more than any of us did. You see they were near of an age and all their tastes went together. Eve was almost heartbroken when we knew that Tom was gone."

"I am sure she was," said Austin, and he said it with such a tender tone that I seemed to love him all at once in a great gush of feeling such as I had never known before.

"Oh, Mr. Gray, you would have liked Tom!" I exclaimed, impulsively. "He was such a dear, dear boy. Everybody loved him, and when he died the Colonel wrote that he was loved and regretted by all ranks of his regiment. And he was so jolly and cheery, such fun and ready for everything that came along."

"And his regiment?"

"He was in the 26th Hussars," I replied.

"My poor little darling," he said kindly. "It must have been terrible for you all." And then he went on talking about Tom and hearing about all of us until, at last, I asked him if he would like to see my photographs.

He said, promptly, that he would greatly like to see them, and I rose to go and fetch them. But before I could leave him, he pulled me down on to the seat again and told me that there was just one thing that I might do for him before I went.

"I'll do it, if I can," I answered, sitting down again.

"Well, in the first place, I don't like you to go on calling me Mr. Gray—it's—it's unkind."

"I don't mind what I call you," I replied smiling.

"That's good. Then perhaps you won't mind calling me Austin in future."

"Yes, I will call you Austin, with pleasure," I said. "Austin is a very nice name—I like it."

"I like it too, now," he said, as if he had never before thought his name even tolerable. "Then Nancy, what about your people? Am I to say anything to them or not?"

"Yes, I think you had better tell Father as soon as he comes back," I replied. It did not certainly occur to me to dread my father's hearing of the new relations between Austin and me. But his next remark proved that he had a wholesome horror of facing a stern parent.

"Hadn't I better wait till after dinner?" he asked, quite nervously, too. "Unless, indeed, he has got a very good bargain during this pilgrimage."

"Why, he isn't an ogre," I cried.

"No, no, but he may take this all wrong—he may think that—that he does not know enough about me—and—and——"

I laughed outright. "You can refer him to somebody, to your commanding officer, to your lawyer and your banker and the clergyman of your parish," I exclaimed, gaily.

"Oh, yes, yes, of course I can. It was only that I did not know how he might take it personally. Some men, you know, are as charming as charming can be until the unlucky day when you go and ask them for their daughters, and then there are ructions, fearful ructions."

"You are evidently very well versed in the process," I remarked.

He turned sharply round upon me. "Nancy, my little woman, are you jealous?" he asked.

"But of whom?" I cried.

"Of anyone. I mean is your nature a jealous one? Else why did you take me up like that? Will you believe me when I tell you that I never in all my life asked any woman to marry me before?"

"Of course, I will. No, I am not at all jealous by disposition—at least I have never been jealous of my brothers and sisters, and as to anyone else, I have never cared for anyone, so that I could not have been jealous, could I? Still, one cannot tell. I may develop a most fearfully jealous disposition; who knows, who can tell?"

"Heaven forbid!" he ejaculated, feelingly. "Forgive me for the suggestion. I thought it might be so from the way in which you took me up, that was all."

"Well, of course, it was the obvious inference—Oh, here is the Colonel. Well, did you pick up any bargains?" I called out to him.

The Colonel sat down on the seat beside us. "My dear child, that young American is a fool," he remarked, solemnly. "I quite thought that all Americans were as keen as knives after bargains in this sort of thing; but evidently this young fellow does not know Majolica from Capo di Monti."

"He has got bargains," I remarked over my shoulder to Austin. "But, Daddy, dear, why draw out the agony like this? You may just as well let us see the treasures at once, without exciting our curiosity in this way. But it's no use," I continued to Austin, "he always does it; it's part of the business."

However, this time my father did not try to draw out the agony but undid his parcel and showed us what he had got. Don't imagine that it was a smart paper parcel such as you get in England; on the contrary, it was done up in his pocket-handkerchief! He opened it with care and displayed his purchase with pride—"Two lire," he said, simply.

"Oh, nonsense!" I cried. "You are chaffing us, Daddy."

"Two lire, I give you my word," he declared—"And as perfect a specimen as I ever remember to have seen."

His other purchases were equally wonderful both as to quality and cheapness, and I did not wonder that he was so visibly elated. I stayed with them for a few minutes, indeed, until it was time to go and make ready for dinner. And then I left them with a careless excuse, thinking that it would be a good opportunity for Austin to make his confession to Father.

However, when I came down again with Mother, I saw at a glance that he had not said a single word. Father, at the sight of us went quickly indoors with a laughing excuse for his enthusiasm. I looked at Austin.

"I never had a chance of saying a word," he whispered, apologetically. "I assure you I had not a chance of getting a word in edgeways. And now I must be off to dress."

He fled away and I sat down on the seat by Mother. She watched him with thoughtful eyes. "Do you like him, Nancy?" she asked. I don't mean that she asked it in a way at all personal to myself. Not at all; but the whole family were so impressed with my gift of reading people that they all were in the habit of, as it were, asking my thoughts of anyone with whom we were brought into contact.

"Yes, I like him immensely," I replied.

"You have had no feeling about him, nothing unusual?" she asked, half hesitatingly. "I mean in your way, you know."

It was the first time since our dear Tom's death that Mother had ever touched upon the subject of my gift of second sight. "Why do you ask, dear?" I said, gently. "Don't you quite like him?"

"Well, yes—I think I do. But I feel as if I knew something about him, though I don't know what." She spoke uneasily, as if she was somewhat disturbed in mind.

"How odd that you should feel that!" I exclaimed, "because, I, too, feel exactly like that about him. I told him so this afternoon."

"And he said——?"

"Oh, he was really silly about it. He says that he believes we all live many, many times over, up or down in the world according to the way we have last behaved ourselves, and—and he thinks that we, that is, he and I, you know, have met before—many times."

Mother turned and looked at me. "Nancy, my darling, has—that is, does Mr.— at least, is he——"

"Yes, I'm very much afraid he is, dear Mother," I replied. I felt the hot blood mount up to my face as my eyes fell before the look of consternation in hers.

"But has he said anything—anything definite, I mean?" she asked.

"Yes, I'm afraid he has," I admitted.

"My dear, dear child," she whispered, taking my hand and looking at me with all her mother's heart in her sweet eyes. "And you really care for him?"

"Well, I think so," I replied.

"But you ought to be quite quite sure," she exclaimed, quickly. "You know, my darling, that marriage is a very serious thing. It is for life. It is a matter about which you cannot think too long and too earnestly."

"We have seen a good deal of each other, you know, Mother," I replied. "It is not as if we had only known each other so long in London or even at Minchester. Here, living in the same house——"

"They are coming back," my mother broke in. "How quick they have been! And there is the bell."

We all went in together. There were a good many people staying in the hotel, though the American party had gone. Among them was a bride and groom, unmistakably English, very stiff to everyone else and very much wrapped up in each other. And they really were the very spooniest couple I had ever seen. I looked at them and wondered if I should ever feel inclined to look at Austin like that? I think he divined something of what was passing through my mind. "I rather like to see it," he murmured under his breath. "Do you think you will ever look at me like that, Nancy?"

Now the same question had just occurred to me, but when he put it into plain words, the answer came both to him and to my own heart like a flash of lightning. "Never, oh, never!" I replied, decidedly.

He laughed outright. "I don't believe you ever will," he said, with a queer little smile playing about his lips.

"Nor would you like it if I did," I said quickly. "You would despise me in next to no time."

"I should never despise you under any circumstances," he said, very quietly—"I have far too great a reason to do otherwise,"

"How otherwise?" I asked, for girl-like I was proud of my new, nay, my first, lover, and liked to see my bear dance.

He did not reply, but he turned and looked at me in away so marked and with such a blaze in his eyes, that my own fell abashed before him.

CHAPTER XVII.
A RECURRENCE.

Answer me, thou mysterious future, tell me - shall these things be according to my desires? —KAVANAGH.

Behold, we know not anything; I can but trust that good shall fall At last—far off—at last, to all. —*In Memoriam.*

MY father was very much astonished when Austin told him that he wanted to marry me; and he was still more surprised when he gathered that I wanted to marry him. Austin told me afterwards that he had declared me to be a mere child, much too young to dream of anything of that kind for years to come.

Then Austin represented to him that I was by no means such a child as he fancied, that I was quite old enough to have fascinated him and that, so far as he was concerned, the mischief was already done.

The Colonel said that he must see me and talk the affair over with me before he said a single word one way or another. And so the two came out on the terrace together, where Mother and I were walking up and down, and Father, dear Daddy, drew me on one side and, tucking his hand under my arm, said—"My little woman, I want a. word with you. What's this I hear about you and Gray, eh?"

"Well, Daddy, he's very nice, don't you think?" I returned, answering one question by another.

"I don't see that he ails anything," admitted my father, deliberately—"But that is not the chief question. Do you really want to marry him?"

"Yes, if you haven't any particular objection, Daddy," I said, meekly.

"H'm, that means that you intend to, whether I have any objection or not. However, to be serious, Nancy, you are too young, too delicate, to think of marrying yet awhile. By the bye, do you—that is, have you told him anything about your clairvoyance?"

"No, I've never mentioned it. I hate talking about it, and he might quite misunderstand it, and——"

"My dear child," said my father gravely, "if you have any idea in your mind that you will not be obliged to tell him that you are troubled in that way, you may as well dismiss it at once and for ever. It would be impossible, it would be most dishonourable. I could not, would not, be a party to anything of the kind."

"I don't want to conceal it," I replied, quickly. "But don't you see how I hate talking about it? As it is, I always feel myself different to everyone we know, which is perfectly horrid and annoys me beyond measure. But to tell someone of it myself, and someone to whom it might make all the difference in the world—why, I could not do it, Daddy, and that's all about it."

"Then you don't mind my telling him?" my father asked, in a greatly relieved tone.

"Not at all; only, need you tell him quite everything that I have seen? The fact that I am afflicted in this way may be more than enough to set him altogether against me——" but all the same, in my heart of hearts, I did not think that it would do anything of the kind.

"I'll tell him the bare facts—" said Father, promptly.

We walked back then and finding Austin alone on the terrace we all sauntered back again together, I walking between them. We said nothing out of the ordinary until we had reached the wall of the terrace, when Father almost abruptly turned to Austin saying—"By the bye, Gray, there is one thing which you ought to know about Nancy here before another word is said of the future. She has the second sight."

I am bound to admit that Austin nearly jumped out of his skin! He gave such a start that my hand, which he had made prisoner within his own as soon as we came to a stand-still against the wall, was jerked quite away from him. He captured it again instantly—"Forgive me," he said, in an undertone. Then he turned to my father. "Is that really so, sir?" he said, in the most incredulous tone. "What do you mean by the second sight?"

My father moved uneasily. "Well, she sees things that are happening elsewhere, through the medium of letters or any contact—and like all such mediums, the possession of this gift is a great trouble to her. That is why she has not told you about it before this. We have done everything we possibly could to prevent its becoming known, for it is a great nuisance. Why, a man actually had the impudence to come to the Warren one day to ask her to try and find out who had stolen some bonds of his. And, by Jove, he read me a lecture as long as my arm because I would not let her try the experiment."

"You don't mean it!"

"Yes, I do. And he was a man whom I had never seen in all my life before and he had not even troubled to get a letter of introduction to me."

"But, Colonel Reynard, you don't mean to say, seriously, that you believe in it?" Austin cried, more incredulously than ever.

"I did not believe in it once," my father admitted. "But since Miss Nancy here has taken to manifestations in this way, it is quite impossible not to believe in it, and that profoundly; I only wish that I could disbelieve. I would if I could, I promise you."

Austin turned and looked at me with a smile. "And is that all which you have to urge against our engagement?" he asked.

"She is very young, too young," said my father half-regretfully.

"She will mend of that, sir," said Austin.

"Yes, yes, I know, I know. Well, we must let it stand over for the present. At all events I must stand out for at least a year's engagement. You clearly understand that?"

"Oh, yes, very clearly," replied Austin, holding my hand fast within his own.

"Well," said my father, with a great sigh, "I am going in. Don't keep her out too long." He just touched my shoulder as he passed and went in without ever seeming to think of making any more of a scene than that. You see we were not a particularly demonstrative family, though we were all devotedly attached to each other.

Austin drew away from the blaze of light which came from the hotel. "So it is all right," he said. "My darling, you are mine, all mine now. Let us sit here awhile. Tell me, Nancy, my own, you are glad that your father did not oppose me? Yes, I know that you are glad, only I want to hear you say it again and again. Kiss me, Nancy, my own, my own."

Yes, I was happy, very, utterly happy, as we sat there in the soft Italian night, listening to the ripple of the lapping waters below the terrace, and talking of our love and planning what we should do in the glorious distant future. At last, Austin, after we had been sitting silent for some few minutes, broke the silence.

"My little one," he said, "is it really true that you have this gift?"

"Yes, Austin, it is quite true unfortunately," I said, simply. "I only hope that when I am married it will see fit to leave me. It is a detestable distinction and has brought me nothing but trouble. I hate even to speak of it."

"Will it comfort you to know that I have no faith in it whatever?" he asked. "I don't believe that such a thing exists at all."

"I am glad you do think so," I replied; "I only hope that I shall never convert you."

"You have felt no such experience with me?"

"No. I have seen nothing since I have known you."

"And you would have done—I mean you have naturally been deeply interested in me, if I may say so without seeming too conceited."

"Yes, I have thought of you a great deal. Oh, Austin dear, if you love me, pray that I may never see anything out of the ordinary again, pray with all your might. I shall bless you all my life. I shall love you ten thousand times more if you are able to break this spell which saps my very life. Dear, say that you will do this for me."

"My darling, I will wish and wish and wish as long as I have my consciousness, that I promise you." And I was so overcome by emotion that I could not speak, or do aught but humbly bend and kiss the hand which held my own.

He spoke again presently. "Do you know, my own," he said—he seemed to be never tired of impressing the fact upon me that I was his, of making me feel that I had become one of his possessions—"I thought it was your sister who had this wonderful reputation."

"My sister—Eve!" I exclaimed.

"Yes, Eve," he replied.

"But how did you know anything at all about it?" I asked, in the utmost astonishment.

"Did not you tell me of it?" he asked in turn.

"No, I am sure I never did. We never speak of it, if we can possibly help it. We make it a rule. I am sure I never told you one word about it. I am as sure as I am that I am living at this moment."

"Then someone must have told me. Possibly I heard it during the few days that I was at Minchester. I must have heard you spoken of as a family and have recalled it to my mind somehow or other, by one of those strange freaks of connection by which our brains do contrive to link certain events and persons together. Is it known at Minchester?"

"Known, oh, yes, too well for my peace and comfort. You should see them talking about me when I go to a dance. It's too horrid—I can almost hear what they say. 'Who's the girl in the pink frock? Rather pretty, eh? You might introduce me, old chap; do you a good turn when I get the chance, yes, by Jove!' And then the other moon-faced booby says—'Ah, ya'as—that's Miss Reynard. Ah, something a bit queer about her—sort of witch, don't you know. Only has to look at you to tell you whether you paid for your boots, or when you're going to be hanged for murdering your great-aunt's Tom cat! By Jove, I shouldn't advise you to risk it, old chappie.' And generally, the old chappie does not risk it, but sheers off and stands in a corner for the rest of the evening, staring at me as if he expects me to suddenly mount a broom-stick and fly away to the moon," I ended, in dire disgust.

Austin laughed heartily over this recital of my woes, but all the same he drew me to him and held me protectingly against his side. "Poor little woman! it is hard for you," he murmured, soothingly. "But there, never mind, perhaps you won't be troubled in that way any more. We must get the Colonel to let us be married as soon as possible and not to stand out for that year of which he spoke just now. I should say that when you are married to an unbelieving Philistine like myself, you will have less and less of these disagreeable manifestations. And you know, I must keep to my original belief that there is no such thing, and that mere coincidences have been developed into apparent facts. When I have really seen you do something about which there can be no dispute I may believe in it, but not before, certainly not before."

"I am not at all anxious to convince you," I declared, laughing a little. "My most sincere wish is that I may never know my power again. If I thought that I was sure of that, I should be as happy a girl as you would find on the earth to-day."

I really did feel that I was more free from my power than I had been for years, and I rejoiced to find that my future husband was so sceptical on the subject. I was sure that the very fact of his being so would protect me against, at least, any fostering of my gift.

All the same I had reckoned somewhat without my host, for within a week of my engagement being a settled thing, a singularly strange manifestation came to me. It happened that we were sitting, Austin and I, on the terrace in our favourite seat, talking of what we would do in time to come, when all at once, I held out my hand and said—"Frank—Frank—you mustn't do that. It will go off. You'll be killed to a certainty!"

CHAPTER XVIII.
MISS LORENZI.

The web of our life is of a mingled yarn, good and ill together. —*All's Well that Ends Well.*

And some chance look or tone Lights up with instantaneous ray, An inner world unknown. —LORD HOUGHTON.

I DON'T know whether I have explained already that my brother Frank was just fifteen months older than I was. He had chosen the Navy as his profession, somewhat against the wishes of both our father and mother. You see, Mother was used to the Army and it seemed a perfectly natural thing for her boys to go in for that and to follow in their father's footsteps; while to her, the Navy seemed a cruelly unnatural kind of life, with many hardships and dangers which had not their corresponding advantages. To Father, on the other hand, the Navy seemed a sheer waste of a smart young fellow, who might reasonably look for advancement in the sister-service. However, nothing would serve Frank but the Navy and so into the Navy he went, getting a nomination from an old friend of Father's, who was one of the Sea-Lords, and, of course, carried such things about in his pocket, ready to give away to the young sons of his old friends.

But that was a long time ago; Frank was twenty at the time of which I am speaking, and a fine strapping young fellow, very like what dear old Tom wag at his age. For some time he had been with the Mediterranean Fleet, but since we had been abroad he had been transferred to one of the guard-ships off the East Coast. On the whole, Frank had not been pleased at the change; he loved the gay life which seemed to follow the Fleet wherever it went and we fancied that on the Guard-ship he found himself very small potatoes indeed, though, as Father said, it was a good thing for him if he was so.

Well, on that particular evening, when Austin and I were sitting out on the terrace at Naples, I suddenly saw Frank just in front of me. It seemed as if I was no longer at Naples but in a narrow street and in a half light. It looked like an English street, and I saw Frank, wearing uniform, and another young man with him, come along quite slowly and as if they were not going anywhere definite but were sauntering round to see what they could see. They had come about half down the street towards me, when I noticed something like a parcel lying just under the wall of a large house, and from which smoke was coming. The man with Frank pointed it out, and Frank immediately went towards it, as if to look at it more closely. The other tried to pull him back, but Frank wrenched himself free of him and tried to stamp out the fuse which was steadily burning. It was then that I involuntarily called out to him as if he had been close to me. . . . The next moment there was a burst of flame and smoke and then everything was hidden from my sight by dense volumes of smoke rising to the very skies!

When I came back to myself, Austin was holding me in his arms and several ladies were trying to restore me from what I knew must have been a long faint. I struggled up and looked at the people around us. "Did I faint? It was very stupid of me," and then a remembrance of what had happened came back to me and I am afraid I was weak enough to go into hysterics.

To my dying day I shall never forget what followed. Austin took hold of my arm and told me in a steady measured sort of voice that I was to stop making that noise immediately. "You can stop this minute if you choose," he said sternly. "And you must choose to do it at once. Do you hear me, Nancy?"

And the queerest thing of all was that I did stop, almost on the instant. I sat up and someone brought some water which Austin held to my lips, saying "Drink a little." I drank it as if I had been some wooden dummy. A lady near took hold of my hand and began to stroke it gently down, but Austin stopped her saying, firmly, "Don't coddle her, please; it will only make her feel more inclined to give way and I know she hates making a scene like this. Now, Nancy, do you think you could walk up and down a little?"

His suggestion was put in the form of a request, but I could not have disobeyed the implied command if my very life and soul had depended on it. I, with his help, got on my feet and began to move slowly along, feeling as if my legs were made of pith and my brain was like the tide, on the ebb and flow. Austin held his arm round me and supported me along until I really began to feel less wobbling than I had done on first getting up. I heard someone whisper as we moved away from the seat—"What a brute! Poor girl, it will be but a sorry time she'll have with him." Yet, I did not feel that Austin was hard or brutal at all . . . He was quite right when he said that I hated making scenes; I did hate anything of the kind and I loved him better than I had ever done for being sensible enough to save me from making one then, and by so doing frightening my mother almost out of her senses.

As we drew near to the place where we had been sitting, he stopped and asked me if I would have another taste of water, and when I said yes, two ladies asked me if I was feeling better?

Austin answered for me. "Oh, yes, she is much better, are you not, dearest?"

"Oh, yes, very much better," I replied.

"The fact is," Austin continued, "Miss Reynard was upset by something and is most anxious that her mother should not know that she was ill. Mrs. Reynard is not in very good health and is easily depressed, so please do not speak of this."

"Oh, but don't you think Mrs. Reynard ought to know?" a lady began when I broke in—

"Please do not say anything to my mother about it," I said eagerly. "She has been in such bad health since my brother died out in India last year and it would do no good. I will go in and tell old Nurse about it. She will know just what to do for me—though indeed, there is nothing to be done. I got a little upset, that was all. I think I will go in now, Austin," I added, turning to him.

We did go in and I found old Nurse and told her all that I had seen. "My lamb," she said, for she still kept to the old terms of endearment—"say never a word to the dear Mistress till Mr. Gray has sent a telegram home to find out if aught has happened amiss to Master Frank. You don't seem to have seen the actual happening, not as you did when our dear Master Tom was taken. Don't delay a minute, sir; send a message off and find out how things are with him. Eh, but I doubt the dear Mistress has a heavy blow waiting for her."

"I'll send off at once," said Austin, "but from whom shall I send it? If I put my own name, the people who get my wire may say, 'What the deuce has this fellow got to do with it?' And if I send in your father's name, the answer will naturally come to him and so the shock be worse to them both than if we had told them what had happened."

"Then send in my name and tell the people not to send the answer in as if it was quite an ordinary thing," I suggested. "If necessary tell the landlord just what has happened."

"Good. I'll go and send it off at once. But mind, Nancy, so far, I don't believe there is anything in it. It was nothing but imagination, nothing else."

"And you will never know how earnestly I hope and pray you may prove to be right," I said, as he departed.

But Austin did not prove to be right. The answer came in due course and he brought it to me in our sitting-room where I was lying on the sofa, old Nurse sitting beside me. "Now, my child," Austin said, coming cheerfully in—"here is the answer. Shall I open it or will you?"

"You do it," I returned, for I began to feel sick and queer again and the room began to spin slowly round me.

He tore open the envelope and glanced hastily over the contents of the enclosure, uttering an astonished "By Jove," as he did so. "No, don't look so alarmed, my darling," he said hurriedly . . . "It's not so bad as you think. Your brother has had the kind of danger you feared, but he was scarcely hurt at all by the accident. Here, read the telegram for yourself." He held the paper out to me and I took it. It was quite long for a telegram and ran thus:

"Partly true. Was in explosion but not hurt. On no account let Mother be frightened. Am writing.—Frank."

The relief was simply enormous, and I had to cry a little on Nurse's shoulder before I could collect myself enough to comment on the more than welcome message.

"What a lucky thing that Mother and the Colonel went that expedition to-day," I managed to say at last.

"Yes; I suppose you will tell them about this when they get home," remarked Austin.

I looked up at him in astonishment. "Why, Austin, we none of us ever kept anything from Mother in all our lives," I exclaimed. "Of course, I shall tell her about it. She would never forgive me if I did not. And you see," I added, in an undertone, "I was right about it. I have never been wrong yet, never."

"Yet you have seen nothing to warn you against me," he said teasingly.

"My lamb, would you like a cup of nice fresh tea?" asked Nurse, at that moment. Nurse had a code of manners quite her own. When any of us ailed anything, she invariably addressed us in the way in which she had been accustomed to address us in the old days of our childhood. On ordinary occasions, she called us by the prefix of Master or Miss.

"I should like some tea, Nurse," I replied. And she, dear old soul that she was, went bustling out of the room to see after it.

"You didn't answer my remark," said Austin, holding my hand and looking searchingly at me.

"No, of course not. You know there is nothing to find out about you," I said, laughing in return. "But depend upon it, I should have been sure to find it out if there had been. I am a most uncanny person to know."

It was nearly an hour after this that my father and mother came home. They had been on a curio-hunting expedition to a little town a few miles from Naples, where as Austin had consolingly told them on leaving, they might reasonably expect to be stabbed in the back with a knife, for the mere offence of possessing a little more of this world's goods than their neighbours for the time being. However, they came triumphantly back all safe and sound and laden with treasures, all immense bargains, of course.

I broke the news to Mother in the gentlest possible way, so as not to alarm her, telling her at the beginning that I had something to tell her but that she had no need to be alarmed. "You have been seeing again," she exclaimed nervously.

"Dear Mother, you need not be frightened. . . . Austin sent a wire home at once and all is well; what I saw was terrifying, but Frank has come to no harm." I then told her everything, except that I had fainted and half-scared Austin and everyone out of their wits.

I scarcely know how it was but I soon found out that Austin was very far from popular among the people staying in the hotel. I might have been wrong, of course, but somehow, I could not help thinking that it was chiefly on account of his firmness in dealing with my threatened attack of hysterics which had prejudiced everyone against him. And, really, when you come to think of it, a more silly objection could not possibly have been taken to any man in the world. But then most people are more or less prejudiced by foolish things, and the people whom we knew at Naples were evidently no exception to the usual run of other people in that respect. Up to that time we had all been very friendly together, not intimate, but still, friendly enough to sometimes make excursions together and to tell one another where we had been and what we had bought.

But now, all that was changed. Whenever Austin joined any group, it somehow melted away, and whenever I was walking with him I used to catch such glances of dislike and apprehension that I was first annoyed and then intensely amused thereby. Austin himself too noticed it. "I don't know what's amiss with the people here," he said to me one day. "They're a most unsociable odd three-cornered sort of lot, and they do cast such sour looks at me that I feel I shall have to do something to justify the character they've evidently given me."

"Oh, you need not trouble to do that," I returned with a laugh, "they have already got the something."

"But what in the wide world have I done to offend their high and mightinesses?" he demanded with a perfectly astonished face.

"Well, I don't really know, because, of course, not a soul has dared to say a single word , to me on the subject, but I think—and I feel quite sure that I'm right—that you upset them all by being so sharp with me that day when I saw that affair with Frank, If you had gone off your head and coddled me up and let me get a good downright fit of hysterics, they would have thought you the perfection of a sweetheart. Now I, on the contrary, who simply loathe giving way to weakness and should have hated myself if I had made a scene, think you quite perfection as you are. You cannot please everyone in this world."

"No, by Jove, and that's true," he exclaimed vexedly. "On my word I'd like to——But there, what's the good even of saying what I would like to do? You are satisfied that what I did was for the best and all the others may go to perdition for aught I care to the contrary. Yet it seems hard that a man should be branded as a kind of double-distilled brute because he does the only sensible thing that is to be done in a case of emergency."

"Oh, what does it matter what these people think? They are nothing to us or we to them, and, for my part, I never want to be anything to them. Next week we go home and we shall probably never meet again. I am sure I hope not. By the bye, I brought down those photographs that I promised to show yon. Let us look at them now."

I had been so long spending a greater part of my life in moving about that I had never possessed an album in which to keep the few portraits without which I did not care to go anywhere. Instead of that I had a neat leather box, with my initials emblazoned on one side in gold. This was just of a size to hold about twenty cabinet portraits, and these I turned out for his edification. The first one that he took up was a splendid likeness of our dear Tom. "That's a good-looking chap," he said, as he looked at it.

"That's Tom, my dear brother—the one who died last year," I said. "Is he not handsome? And he was such a dear dear boy; you don't know what it was to us to lose him."

It was very strange but, as I spoke, the well-known white mist began to form in front of my eyes and I felt myself slipping off into the state in which I always saw things. Slowly a vision pieced itself together before me and I became aware that I was once more looking on a familiar scene, that of Mr. Warrender's quarters in Danford Barracks.

"Yes, it must have been an awful shock to you," said Austin at that moment. He spoke in cool unconcerned conventional tones and that somehow put my vision entirely to flight. For the first time in all my life, I had seen a vision without attempting to communicate it to those about me and, indeed, without my companion being aware that I was affected in that way. The feeling was most strange to me. I felt as if my heart was weighed down by a mighty secret and yet for worlds I could not have revealed it to Austin. He went on talking and asking questions and making remarks about the photographs and was quite unconscious that anything out of the ordinary run of events had happened to me.

It was only a couple of days after this, that my people somewhat suddenly decided to start on our journey homewards. We had got as far as Milan and determined to stay there for a few days, as we had fallen in with some charming friends whom we had met several years before while staying on the Riviera. These people, a Mr. and Mrs. Johnstone, with two young daughters and a pleasant friend who was travelling with them, were quite overjoyed to see us again and begged us not to go on as we had intended to do, but to put in a few days and talk the past over again.

My father and mother consented, and so we lingered for a while longer under the pleasant Italian skies and made excursions to various points of interest in company with each other. And the last night, just after dinner, we were all sitting in the great entrance of the hotel taking our coffee and chatting, when the lady who was travelling with the Johnstones—by name, Miss Lorenzi, said to me suddenly, "Miss Reynard, you are a clairvoyante."

I was so taken aback that I stammered out a faint admittal of the impeachment, though I could have bitten my tongue off as soon as the words had passed my lips. "But what makes you say so?" I asked, trying to hide my vexation.

"Because I felt what Mr. Gray was thinking through you," she replied. "Of course, you have the look of a clairvoyante, but until a moment ago, I was not sure of it."

"And what was I thinking of?" Austin demanded.

"Oh, a clairvoyante has no right to publish the thoughts of others," she said quite gravely.

"Give me a clue," he urged.

"I will. You were thinking of someone in India," said Miss Lorenzi, without the least hesitancy.

"By Jove, so I was," he exclaimed. Then turned to me. "Dearest," he said, "I yield to you. I am more than convinced. But how do you account for this, that although Miss Reynard and I have been—and very naturally—thrown a great deal together during the last few weeks she has never seen anything unusual about me, has never once been influenced in any way by me? If she were a true clairvoyante, would she not by this time have discovered everything about me that has ever happened? Would she not have told my thoughts sometimes?"

Miss Lorenzi turned and looked fixedly at him. "Do you know anything about the second sight?" she asked rather abruptly, "I should imagine not—but, do you?"

"Not a single thing," replied Austin, "that is, excepting what I have gathered from Miss Reynard here. Why do you ask?"

"I had a reason," she replied. "Well, it is evident to me that you do not know the subject, for if you had, you would know first of anything, *that a clairvoyante cannot see anything for herself.* "

CHAPTEE XIX.
AT HOME!

Bright was her face with smiles, and words of welcome and gladness, Fell from her beautiful lips.

—Evangeline,

As lamps burn silent with unconscious light, So modest ease in beauty shines most bright, Unaiming charms with edge resistless fall, And she who means no mischief does it all.

—HILL.

YES, that was what Miss Lorenzi said—"A clairvoyante cannot see anything for herself!" Nobody spoke for a moment and I sat staring at her like one fascinated. I seemed to know she was right, for she spoke with the solemn and pronounced manner of one who knew intimately what she was talking about.

It was Austin who first broke the silence. "I think," he said, "that we don't any of us quite follow you. How do you mean cannot see for herself?"

"Just in this way," Miss Lorenzi replied. "Miss Nancy here is a clairvoyante—

she is engaged to you and perhaps because she sees nothing of your inner life she may imagine that you have no inner life to see, that you are all fair and above-board and that there are no stories in your past which——" However, there she broke off short and looked at him. Austin went perfectly livid, but he tried to laugh off the effect of her words.

"Really, Miss Lorenzi, you are most flattering; you——"

"Stay," said she quietly. "I never said that there *were* any stories in your past into which you would not like your friends to enquire; I never said that you *had* an inner life or that all was not fair and above board. You jump to conclusions too quickly."

He calmed down instantly. "No, no more you did. But your manner seemed to imply as much, and to tell the truth, that is the one point upon which I am touchy. I beg your pardon."

Miss Lorenzi smiled and said there was no occasion for that, and we by common though tacit consent began to talk of other things. We separated soon after and, though we breakfasted together the following morning, we did not in any way revert to the subject which had seemed so inclined to be unfortunate the previous evening.

I am sure that Austin was very glad to be free from any further chance of discussing that particular subject with Miss Lorenzi. We had a compartment to ourselves and naturally Mother and the Colonel sat at one end and Austin and I sat at the other, thus occupying the four corners. We had not been more than half an hour or so on our way, when Austin asked me if I had felt anything of Miss Lorenzi's power of clairvoyance?

"I mean, does she strike you as being clairvoyante?"

"No, not particularly," I replied. "Why, what makes you ask?"

"I wanted to know, that was all. You know, I don't believe she was right in what she said about no clairvoyante being able to see for herself. Do you?"

"I don't know. She spoke as if she knew what she was talking about," I returned. "But why worry about it? I don't believe you have a past, Austin, and it does not matter if anyone else does, does it?"

"Oh, but it's not that; it's not that at all," he said quickly. "Of course, it is horrid to feel that a doubt may have been put into your mind and that may blossom and bear fruit some day. Besides, your father and mother may feel that they don't know enough of me. . . ."

"My dear boy," I replied, in the same undertone in which he had spoken—"I wouldn't trouble about that, if I were you. If my father has even the faintest shadow of a doubt, he won't in the least hesitate to ask you to explain every circumstance of your life right up to the present time."

"But I've knocked about the world so much——"

"Nonsense! You can give him a dozen references, any one of which will be enough to set any lingering doubt he might have at rest. You can tell him who your school-master was——"

"I was educated at Harrow," he said, in rather an offended voice.

"How odd that I should never have asked you or you have told me where you were educated," I cried, with a laugh. "Well, then you can tell whose time and whose house you were in. And, you can give him the name of your Vicar—and your Banker and the Colonel of your regiment—why, there are heaps of people to whom you can refer him. Don't give a second thought to that Miss Lorenzi. I believe she is nothing but a fraud. Yes, I do really, for I feel sure I should have known it in some way if she had been as I am."

"You really think so?"

"Yes, I do really. I feel sure of it. Oh, dont think about her any more. By the bye, did she give you the clue to what you were thinking of?"

"Yes, she did."

"Ah, well, I daresay she is to a certain extent clairvoyante, a sort of medium; but I have never been able to tell people what they are thinking about and I don't believe I ever shall be able to do so. Let us talk about other things. I wonder, yes, I do wonder very much how you will like my sisters."

"Your sisters . . . that is Mrs. Dagenham and——"

"And Eve. Eve is charming. I think you saw Madge's portrait the other day. It was among those that I shewed you."

"And why did you not shew me Eve's portrait?" he asked.

"For a very good and excellent reason, because Eve has never had her photograph taken."

"Not really?" he cried, in great astonishment. "And is she—I mean is there any reason why she should not have had her photograph taken?"

"Not at all. Eve is very good-looking, very much better looking than I," I replied. "No, but she is not like the ordinary run of girls; she hates the idea of having it taken, and consequently it has never been done. They are both quite out of the common run, my sisters; at least, they both were till Madge got a baby . . . that did turn her head a bit, but I should think that will wear off after a while, when she gets more used to it.'

"Why, is she so fond of this baby?" he asked.

"She adores it," I replied solemnly. "Fond is no word, unless you choose to use it in another sense. Still, they are both charming and I should not be a bit surprised if you fall over head and ears in love with Eve, not a bit."

"I shall not do that," he said, without in any way reciprocating my gay tone. "Your sister may be the most beautiful woman in the world, but all the beauty that ever I saw could not possess the attraction for me that you do, my Nancy. Don't you understand that?"

I suppose I did or thought that I did, which amounted to pretty much the same thing, for the time-being at least. So I smiled back at him and told him in various ways that I was delighted to hear that it was so, and added that I hoped it would always be the same with him.

"My little Nancy," he said, taking my hand under cover of a week-old newspaper. "You seem to have a few doubts of my constancy but never to have any of your own. How do you know that you may not entirely change your mind and give me the go-by?"

"I don't think so," I said wisely. "It is possible, of course, but I think it is very improbable."

He seemed to be convinced; at all events, he said no more on the subject and we discussed entirely different things until we arrived at Turin, where we intended to remain for a couple of days. I liked Turin exceedingly, though several people had told us that it was not worth our while to break our journey there. We did so, because my mother was not very strong, and the Colonel thought it would in every way be better and easier for her if we took a week or so on the way, than if we rushed through in a single day.

We did not fag much at sight seeing. We had seen so many picture-galleries and old churches that we did not any of us care about seeing any more. So we walked about the streets and drove around the environs, half inclined to wish that we were going up among the snows of the everlasting Alps, instead of going home to the common-place life of an English country town. However, we had promised those who were at home that we would be back by a certain date and we had practically no choice but to steadily turn our faces homewards.

We left Turin early in the morning, having stayed there two nights, and, just at the last minute, Mother said she would rather go straight through to Paris, and as Father had no choice in the matter other than for her comfort, he decided at once to do so. I firmly believe that she had an eye to her presents and wanted to have every available moment for choosing them in the gay city where good Americans go when they die.

So we went from Turin straight to Paris, and for my part, I was very very glad to find myself there. "I propose we come to Paris for our honeymoon, Austin," I said to my sweetheart, when we were sauntering along the Boulevard des Italiens the morning after our arrival.

"It wouldn't be half a bad idea," he replied. "That is, if the Colonel really does insist on our waiting a whole year, which, by the bye, between ourselves, Nancy, is a fearful nuisance. But if he gives in and gracefully consents to our getting married in July or August, why, Paris will be simply out of the question."

"Yes, I suppose so," I said regretfully, feeling half inclined to wish for a minute that my father might hold out for the last time . . . "Oh, do stop, I must look in this window. Oh, look at this, Austin, did you ever see anything so charming as that?"

The object of my admiration was a small bronze of great beauty, lightness and delicacy, a mere trifle, yet one which struck the eye and arrested the attention where many a more important subject would have failed to do so.

As he did not answer, I looked round, just in time to see him putting his hat on his head again, having evidently taken it off in order to salute someone passing by. "Is that someone you know?" I asked.

"Oh, no one in particular," he replied, "Only an Army man I know slightly. He saw that I was with a lady."

"What is his name?" I asked, watching the man walking briskly along.

"His name? Well, on my word, I forget," said Austin, turning back to look in the window again. "One meets so many fellows mixed up with the Service at one time or other, you know, and it's quite impossible to remember them all. By the bye, Nancy, what were you looking at just now and admiring so rapturously?"

I pointed out the little bronze and Austin after looking at it for a minute or so, said . . . "My dear child, you have as pretty a taste in art as anyone could wish. Let us go in and see if it is within our means. I should like you to have it."

"Not if it's too expensive," was my warning, as we passed into the shop.

However, he decided that it was quite within his means and bought it. As a matter of fact, it was about seven pounds and I thought it rather an extravagance, but Austin quite pooh-poohed the idea and told me it was mine. "Let us take a Victoria back," he said, when we got out on to the boulevard again.

"But, my dear boy, we have only just come out," I expostulated, for I had no notion of coming to Paris for a few days to stay stuck in a stupid hotel all the time.

"Oh, well, let us go for a little drive first," he suggested. "I don't feel like walking about much to-day. The sun is so fearfully hot. Let us go to the Madeleine and get some flowers. All women want to go and buy flowers when they come to Paris."

I agreed to this and he hailed a victoria which was passing by. We drove away in the direction of the Madeleine and then I chanced to look at him. "Have you a headache, Austin?" I asked.

"No. Why, what makes you ask?"

"Because you are so white and you look so . . . so . . . done up," I returned.

"To tell you the truth I feel so," said he, "and I cannot think why I should, for I have had a most tremendously easy time of late. I shall be all right presently. Besides, you know, dearest, Paris is essentially a place to live luxuriously in, and Shanks's nags is not the most luxurious mode of transport that can be imagined."

Of course, his explanation was a perfectly reasonable one and his colour came back before we reached the Madeleine, so that I did not then give another thought to the incident but applied myself to the business in hand of buying flowers and fruit.

We were rather reckless about victorias during the rest of the time we were in Paris, and really I too was glad of it, for Paris was fearfully hot although it was only April. Still, heat or no heat, we had a lovely time and I enjoyed every minute of it.

We stayed five days in Paris and then crossed to London, where we put up at

Father's favourite hotel and prepared for a few days of theatre going, with a visit or two to the tailor's on his part.

I did enjoy London, even more than Paris, only when we were in Paris I thought that I enjoyed it more than I had ever done London, so perhaps there was very little to be said for the state of my taste at that particular time. For one thing, Austin had preferred to wait till we got to London before he bought me any jewelry. Even my engagement ring he had sent to London for, for as he said when you were dealing with London tradespeople for things about which you understood nothing, you were tolerably safe. And he did give me such a lot of presents during those few days, I more than once felt obliged to cry, "Hold, enough," which is not the usual way with young girls, who love pretty things just as much as anyone else.

We did fill those few days, as full as ever they would go. I seemed to live through a lifetime and I liked Austin better every day that went by. And, you know, there were times when I was not so rare of my own feelings, at least not exactly that, but there were times when I could not for the life of me think of anything to say next. Now and again it would occur to me that there must be something wrong about me or about him or about us both, for it seemed so unnatural for two people who were supposed to be madly in love with each other—an old phrase of Madge's, by the bye—to sit for ever so long without speaking, for the girl to be racking her brains for a suitable subject of conversation and for the man to say suddenly apropos of nothing at all, "I beg your pardon, my darling, what did you say?" . . . thus shewing plainly that his thoughts had been for ever so long far far away.

Of course, these occasions were not frequent, but when they did happen, they always worried me dreadfully. You see I could only go back for the etiquette of deportment at such a time to my eldest sister's behaviour under similar circumstances. Now Madge, no matter who the man of the moment might be, never seemed to be in want of a subject to talk to him on. I have seen Madge go away down the garden with that stiff gaby, James Allistair, talking as fast as ever her tongue could slip off the words. I am sure that James Allistair never had a word to throw at a dog, but he always had plenty to say to her, plenty and to spare.

However, I never wanted for words during the time that we were in London, never. And as I said before, I thoroughly enjoyed our stay from beginning to end.

And at last we left dear London behind us and were fairly started on our journey homewards. You know it is a long journey from London to Minchester, the weather was hot and trying and I was very very glad when I found that we were drawing near our destination.

"I cannot tell you how glad I shall be to get home." I said to Austin.

"You are tired?" he said, gently. "I quite expect that you will laugh at me, Nancy, when I confess to you that I am getting quite nervous at the idea of meeting all your people."

"But there is no such great all," I replied, laughing at the notion of anyone being nervous at the thought of meeting my two dear sisters and dear old Geoffrey Dagenham. "Certainly, nothing to be nervous about. They are all charming and will be delighted to meet you. Besides, it is not as if it were my father or mother—then you might have an excuse to feel nervous. But the others have no real say in the matter. And, of course, you did see Dick in Town."

"Yes, but it is an awful ordeal."

"Not a bit more than if you were taking me to meet your people," I declared.

"But practically, I have no people," he returned, "and charming and happy as family life is, there are advantages attached to the fact of being almost relationless. Especially, when one is about to be married."

"Oh, I don't mind your having no near relations," I said, smiling, "you will be the more able to value mine. Why, here we are. How quickly the last little bit has gone by."

"There's Geoffrey on the platform . . . . and Madge," said the Colonel at that moment. "Hollo," he called out, as he let down the window. "Hi, here we are. How are you?"

In a moment Madge had rushed up to the carriage and without waiting for any of us to alight, jumped up and caught Mother in her arms.

"My dear, dear Mother," she cried; then turned to me . . . "Why, Nancy, I have never seen you look so blooming in all my life. And this is Mr. Gray. How are you? I'm delighted to see you."

And then we all got out and stood in a group on the platform while our luggage was being put together. We had sent most of it down on our arrival in London so that we had only our Town luggage with us, not to mention many cardboard boxes containing recent purchases in the way of clothing.

"We brought the break over," Madge continued, "for we thought we might find you so hung around with parcels that we could not possibly get into either the stanhope or into the flies. Come, dear," putting her hand under Mother's arm, "let us leave the others to do the best they can."

We all drove back to the Warren together, and I saw that Austin was immensely taken by my sister, and also that, Madge and Geoffrey were very much pleased with him. This alone was highly satisfactory, for it is pleasant to find that your choice has been justified, particularly by those whose opinion you value.

"By the bye, why did not Eve come to meet us?" I asked as we turned in at the gate of the Warren.

"She has had a dreadful cold the last few days, and though she is better," Madge replied, "I persuaded her that she had best stay at home, for you know what a draughty place the station is and you might have been ever so long getting your things together."

As she spoke a turn in the drive brought us within sight of the house and I saw Eve, with a white lace wrap round her head, come hastily out into the porch. In a moment we had drawn up at the door, and the next instant I was clasped in my sister's arms.

For a minute or two all was confusion and a perfect babel of tongues, the servants all came out and there was a general handshaking and greeting. Then I turned to see what had become of Austin, fearing that he would feel left out in the cold, when I found that he was staring straight at Eve, the very picture of uncanny fascination!

CHAPTER XX.
THE INEVITABLE.

Fortune brings in some boats that are not steer'd. —***Cymbeline.***

Alas for Virtue, when Torments, or contumely, or the sneers of erring-judging men, Can break the heart where it abides! Alas! if love, whose smile makes this obscure world splendid, Can change, with its false times and tides, Like hope and terror— Alas for Love. —SHELLEY.

WHEN I saw how Austin was staring with all his eyes at my sister Eve, I turned involuntarily and looked at her. To my surprise I found that Eve had grown quite white, white to the very lips, and that her eye-lids had drooped so that her eyes could not be seen. I was so puzzled that I scarcely knew what to do. Then I remembered that I had not introduced him to Eve and thought perhaps she was embarrassed thereby, though why that should be so in a free-and-easy family like ours, I simply could not tell. However, I had no idea of my future husband and my sister remaining as strangers to one another, so I went across to Austin and said, "I want to introduce you to my sister, Eve."

He gave a great jump, as if I had startled him suddenly, but pulled himself together and said, in just his ordinary tones—"Yes, yes, do introduce me, darling."

So I took him over to where Eve was standing. "Eve, this is Mr. Gray. I hope for my sake that you will like each other."

The words were no sooner out of my mouth than I felt that I had said the wrong thing. Why it was wrong, I did not know; but it was wrong, of that I was certain. Eve looked up at him for just a minute, a mere flash of a glance, and then immediately dropped her eyes again. She held out her hand and Austin took it and kept it fast in his own until, indeed, she drew it away. "I am delighted to meet you," said he, in a voice which was new to me. "May I also echo your sister's wish and hope that you will not dislike me?"

Then Eve looked up again. "Of course, I shall not dislike you," she said, and she seemed to say it with an effort. "What an absurd idea. Why, we have been quite anxious to see you, Mrs. Dagenham and I; we have talked of you so much."

I thought that I had better go away and leave them to become better acquainted, and as I moved away I heard him say in a very low tone—"And I did not know of the honour . . . and happiness." He spoke the two last words in such an undertone that they only just caught my ear, indeed, I was not quite sure whether he really said them or whether I had fancied it. It seemed such an unlikely thing for him to say, for Austin was not a gushing kind of person, quite the contrary, in truth.

I made my way over to where Madge was sitting close to Mother and just pouring out the tea. "My dear child," she whispered to me as I sat down, "I congratulate you a thousand times, he is quite charming."

"I'm glad you like him," I replied, wondering the while what could possibly have possessed Eve. "He is good-looking, isn't he?"

"Very very good-looking," returned my sister, who with all her devotion to Geoffrey and that baby, had not forgotten what a good-looking man was like. "And so charming too. I think you are very lucky, Nancy, dear, for although a good husband is a very desirable creature, I always think that he is none the worse for being handsome too."

I glanced across to see how the two were getting on. Eve had seated herself on the wide lounge near to which they had been standing, and Austin was standing talking to her, talking away at a great rate too. As I looked she glanced up and with a smile made a gesture to him that he should sit down beside her. He was just about to do so, when he saw me take a cup of tea from Madge, on which he came and took it out of my hand.

"And for whom is this?" he asked.

"For Eve," I replied. "No, she does not take sugar."

I turned back to the table again and went on talking to Madge, and by and by, it being late, we all went our different ways that we might get ready for dinner.

I went of course to my usual room, one that opened out of Eve's. "Well," I said, going in after her. "Tell me, what do you think of him?"

"I think he is exceedingly handsome," said Eve, but she spoke without the smallest enthusiasm and I felt nettled accordingly.

"You don't like him," I blurted out.

Eve turned and flung her arm round me. "Oh, my dear dear Nancy," she said, in a shaking voice, "forgive me, I cannot go into raptures over anyone who is going to take you right away from us. Mr. Gray *is* very handsome and he seems to be a most charming man too; but I have a feeling, I cannot help feeling that he will part us from each other somehow."

"My dear Eve," I cried in direst dismay, for this was a wholly unlooked for catastrophe and one on which I had therefore not reckoned, "don't, pray don't begin with any such horrid idea. It's true that we are not going to live in Minchester or anywhere hereabouts, but we shall be within reach and there is no reason why you and I should be any different to each other now than we have been before. You have never felt any differently about Madge. Why should you do so in my case?"

"Nancy dear," said Eve, still keeping her arm around me. "It was different then. We were very young when Madge was married, and after all you and I have been nearer to each other, more to each other than ever she and I have been. We have been through sorrow together and that alone makes everything quite different. As it is, I feel that we shall never be the same again, you and I, never quite the same again."

She spoke with inexpressible sadness and held me tightly to her.

"Don't take any notice of me," she said after a minute or two. "I am silly and weak to-night. Don't let me spoil your first evening at home, and when you are so happy too. I'm a fool, but I never thoroughly knew it before."

"But I can't think what you have been doing to yourself, Evie," I cried. "I never saw you in this sort of way before, you are getting positively pessimistic."

Eve caught me up instantly. "Bless me," she cried, with a sudden change of tone. "Where did you pick up that long learned word, I wonder? Has the incomparable Austin been putting the finishing touches on your education already?"

"Don't be silly," I answered laughing, for it was a perfect blessing to see her somewhat more like herself. "It's an ordinary word enough and a most useful one. Well, I must fly and get ready at once or I shall be late."

"Yes, go this minute; don't be late for anything," cried my sister, gently pushing me out of the room.

I was late and I applied myself to the task of dressing for dinner with all possible despatch, and when I was ready I went back into Eve's room to see if she was dressed also, so that we might go downstairs together. To my surprise, she was standing before the chest of drawers resting her head upon her hands. I shut the door softly and stole away.

The only person that I found in the drawing-room was Madge. And I tackled her on the subject at once. "I say, Madge," I said, plunging straight into the question which was puzzling me so woefully. "I want to ask you a plain question."

"Then ask it," said Madge, in the most ordinary every day tones.

"Well, it is just this. Has Eve been fretting at all about my being married?"

"Eve! No, not the least in the world. Why, you little conceited thing, of course, not. Eve is simply delighted over the whole affair."

"She has a very queer way of showing it, that's all I can say," I remarked drily. "She is down in a fit of the worst blues that I have ever seen her in, says we shall never be the same again and a lot more in the same strain. And when I looked into her room just now, she was standing up in front of the chest of drawers resting her face in her hands and looking the very picture of disconsolate wretchedness. Of course, we all know it is rather a wrench to leave home, and a wrench when others go; but I have only just come back again and we are not going to be married for ages. Why, Eve may be married herself long before I am."

I heard Madge laugh and then the most extraordinary thing happened. I felt my head begin to spin round and the white mist came in front of my eyes which always foretold a vision of some kind. Then a picture began to form slowly, and I saw Eve, my sister, Eve, standing in front of an altar-rail with a white-robed clergyman on the other side of it. I was conscious that there was a bridegroom but the figure was quite obscured by the thick white mist, which shut out the rest of the picture. "Eve is getting married," I said, with a gasp to Madge. "I can see her plainly, she is wearing a grey frock and a grey hat. It is made with a great many little tucks here and there. I cannot see the bridegroom but she is being married, the ring is on. Now she kneels down . . . yes, she is being married. Ah, now it has all gone."

Madge positively shook me in her eagerness. "Nancy, Nancy, they are coming," she cried, "keep this to yourself. Pray, pray, don't say a single word about it. *Madge has got a new grey frock; it is made exactly as you describe and she has a hat to match it.*"

Just then the door opened and Mother came in, followed by Geoffrey and then by Austin, who came straight across the room to me.

"Well, my darling," he said in just his ordinary tones . . . "and have you had anything of a gossip yet?"

I looked at him. I tried to say something but the words died away on my lips and I put my hand into his instead.

"What is the matter?" he asked. "Don't you feel well, dear?"

"Not very. Don't say anything. I shall be all right in a minute," I replied, and even to my own ears, my voice sounded far-away and strange.

Austin looked closely at me. "You have not been seeing things again, have you?" he asked, in a suddenly enlightened way.

"Yes, but nothing horrid," I returned.

"And what is it this time?" he demanded.

"I cannot tell you——"

"Nothing about me, I hope. You know I live in daily, nay, in hourly dread of it," he said, half teasingly.

"Oh, no, nothing about you. Nothing to alarm anyone, only I never see anything without feeling as if it would kill me, never. I hate seeing things," I added vehemently.

As usual, with every moment I felt the influence less and less, and by the time Eve came downstairs, I wag almost myself again. Mercifully, no one else noticed that anything had happened to me, and Madge kept her own counsel about it. So I escaped observation, for which, under the circumstances, I was profoundly thankful.

I never look back to that first evening at home at the dear Warren without a feeling of pleasure mingled with sadness. For Eve, the loved sister and friend of my childhood, the companion of my girlhood, was never quite the same Eve to me again. She had spoken truly when she said that she had a feeling that Austin would part us from each other. So he did, but not in the way in which she imagined. I don't know what could have put it into my head, but I thought that Eve had some kind of a love-affair on hand which had made a difference in her manner towards all of us. Well, perhaps it was the half vision that came to me that put such a thought in my head. Yet Eve was quite her own old self that night and played at round games with the best of us. And so we went to bed and Madge came into our rooms for a long long chat over our hair-brushing. How we talked that night. And how Madge teased me about Austin—"Your young man" as she called him.

And, of course, I had to show them all the beautiful presents he had given me while in Town, and what with one thing and another, it was two o'clock before we parted and got into our respective beds. For my part, I went off to sleep feeling just as happy as I had ever done in my life, quite thinking that the cloud which had seemed to be hanging over Eve, had passed away. Yet with daylight it came back again, and I knew that everything was changed and would never come right again.

Not all in one day, oh, dear no, but from that day things went less smoothly and there was always an undercurrent of unrest and make-believe about us all, though I do think that none of us quite knew why.

For one thing, Austin and Eve avoided each other, yes, I could not shut my eyes to it. Nor could I tell why . . . I only know that they did. And very awkward it was, for Madge and her husband went home after a few days and then we three younger ones were thrown pretty much together. Of course, it was quite natural that Austin should pair off with me, and that Eve should make engagements without either consulting us or taking us into account. Yet when we went out to Dagenham, we equally naturally went together and then the coolness between them was most painfully apparent and to me most embarrassing. I asked Austin about it one day. "Why don't you and Eve like each other, Austin?" I asked bluntly.

"Does Eve dislike me?" he asked, in such a curious tone. "When did she say so?"

"Of course she never said so," I returned, impatiently. "But you don't like each other, you know that as well as I do. Why, you avoid each other like the plague and never speak a word if you can possibly help it."

"I came here to be near you, not to cultivate your sister," he said, after a moment's pause.

I am afraid I was very rude, for I said plump out "Fiddlesticks."

Austin looked up and regarded me with a grave and abstracted gaze.

"Dearest," he said, if you think that I do not pay your sister attention enough——"

I uttered an exclamation of impatience. "Oh, dear, dear, how difficult you both are to manage," I cried. "Really, if I did not know it to be impossible, I should imagine that you were both in love with each other and were pining away from a mistaken sense of honour."

"And yet you insist that we dislike each other," said Austin, in a bantering tone. "You are like all your sex, most inconsistent, my child."

"Well, perhaps I am; I only know that everything is most uncomfortable and changed from what the Warren used to be. Ah, it was jolly in the old old days . . . before poor dear Tom died. Do you know," I continued, "I believe, joking apart, that Eve has never got over the awful shock of Tom's death."

"Was she so fond of him then?" Austin asked, in a somewhat constrained tone.

"Fond of him! Why, she was simply devoted to him. She adored him. Tom and she were the greatest chums that ever were in any family in the world. We thought she would have died when we knew—and so I believe she would have done, if it had not been for our fear that Mother would lose her reason."

He said nothing, but after a little while he put out his hand and took mine. "Darling," he said, in a sort of way as if he had stubbornly made up his mind that he would do something that was not very palatable to him, "I am so sorry about it all. I will try to win your sister's regard . . . if I can."

Yet things got no better after this. True, Austin paid Eve a good deal more attention, but Eve's restrained manner did not relax in the least. I said nothing about it to her. I did not mind asking my lover to be nice to my sister, but I could not quite bring myself to ask my sister to be more kind to my lover. Perhaps I was wrong, but as that was how I felt, I acted on it. So the days went on until Austin's visit had almost come to an end and he began to talk of going back to Town, and he and Eve seemed just as far away from each other as ever.

I confess it troubled me very much. You see, we Reynards had always been such a united family and Madge's husband had always been just like one of ourselves, so that this marked want of friendliness between Austin and Eve was something quite new and altogether detestable. However, the days sped on, and Austin's last one came. Mother had asked Madge and Geoffrey to come over and stay the night and I had promised Madge that I would go back to Dagenham with them for a week or so, after Austin had gone.

We were expecting them every moment and Mother had made me promise—

she being gone for a drive with the Colonel—that if Eve should happen to be out when they came, that I would see that they got some tea as soon as they arrived. Austin and I were in the garden, when I was called in to see someone who had come begging for a little soup for a sick person.

"I won't be more than a minute," I said to him as I went towards the house, and I thought to myself that I would speak about the tea while I was on this errand.

Of course, I was longer than a minute—every body who goes on an errand is. I had to see the poor woman and listen to her tale of woe, suggest a few little dainties in addition to the soup, and then to speak to the parlour-maid about the tea being delayed until Mr. and Mrs. Dagenham's arrival. So it must have been quite half an hour ere I went back to the garden to rejoin Austin.

I did not find him where I had left him, that is under the great tree where we always sat in hot weather; but as I stood there idly cogitating, I caught a glimpse of Eve's white frock just beyond the hedge which shut off the kitchen garden from the lawn. I went towards her, without stopping to think whether she was alone or not and then to my intense surprise saw that she was with Austin, her hands held fast in his, her face downcast, and in his an expression such as I had never brought there!

For a moment I was stunned . . . stunned . . . So ***this*** was the meaning of the avoidance, the coldness, the frozen silence of these two, my sister and my lover. They loved each other and I—I, Nancy Reynard, stood between them!

CHAPTER XXI.
IN THE GARDEN.

Forget your past circumstances, whether they be sorrows or joy. —D. MA-CLAREN.

Somewhere there waileth in this world of ours For one lone soul, another lonely soul, Each chasing each through all the weary hours, And strangely meeting at one sudden goal. —SIR EDWIN ARNOLD.

IT happened that neither Austin nor my sister had heard my footfall on the soft turf. Probably both of them were so taken up with their disturbed feelings that they were more or less blind to outer influences. "Can ***nothing*** be done?" I heard Austin say in a desperate sort of tone.

"Nothing—except to hide it all," said Eve. She spoke in a very firm voice but with unutterable sadness. As for me, I just stood still and listened, the first time in my life that I had ever indulged in or felt inclined to indulge in eavesdropping. But this I felt I had more right to hear than anybody.

"But you know you love me, Eve," he said passionately.

"But she loved you first," answered Eve pitifully and looking up at him again.

"Eve, my love, my love. God help me, I never knew what love was until now." His tone was bitterness itself and he caught her to him with what was almost a cry. I stole lightly away and passed swiftly into the house and up to my own room, leaving them to their brief spell of heartbroken delirium.

So it was all over! Eve had been right and Austin had come to part us, though not as she and I had thought. I might have saved them a few pangs if I had gone boldly forward and told them that I had learned the truth and that I would, not stand in their way. But I wanted to get used to it a little and to make up my mind to bear the wrench of giving him up before I told even the two whom it would most affect.

Looking back, how well I remembered my suggesting that as likely as not he would fall in love with Eve and how he had laughed the very notion to scorn. Yet nevertheless it had come true, that word spoken in jest, and it was Eve whom my Austin loved, not Nancy at all. ***My*** Austin did I say? Why, he was mine no longer but Eve's, all Eve's, and would be Eve's always, whether I chose to set him free of his promise or not. Ay, and I think that was the greatest rub of all, the knowledge that whatever I chose to do, I could not help the one fact, that he was Eve's, all Eve's and would be herd for ever and ever, for all time.

But I never even for a moment thought of accusing Austin and Eve of falseness towards me; and I never thought of keeping him to his word. Oh, no, I had no fancy for a husband who would be a mere shell, who would be mine to all outward semblance and who in heart and soul would irrevocably belong for all time to another. I know that women have done such things as these, and have lived in a hell of jealousy and impotent craving after the unattainable ever after. And much as I had loved and did love Austin, I was not willing to do the one thing which would ruin his whole life. Besides, where would be the sense of keeping a man's hand where one could not have his heart?

I was still in my room when a maid came to tell me that Mr. and Mrs. Dagenham had come. I went straight down to them and explained where Mother and the Colonel were. "You shall have some tea in a minute, dears," I told them. "And tell me, how is the blessed boy?"

Madge gave me some details about the precious boy but then turned and looked at me rather sharply. "Have you been ill, Nan?" she said. "You're surely not fretting about Austin going away?"

"Not at all," I replied promptly, for I was in no way minded to hold myself up as an object of pity to my family.

Just then Austin came in and, after greeting the new-comers, began to help me to pour out the tea, or rather to hand it round. I looked at him when I could, this poor soul just come from the burial of his life's romance. I had never loved him better than now, when I saw him with dark dark shadows under his eyes and lines about his mouth which had grown there in a few short hours. Poor Austin, my heart bled for him, as it ached for myself.

"And where is Evie?" asked Madge presently.

"Oh, she is about somewhere or other," I replied carelessly, leaving any further explanation to come from Austin, who knew better than any of us where Evie was.

But Austin said never a single word, not even that she had been out in the garden since I had been called into the house. Poor fellow, he tried hard to do so but I saw that the words would not come in spite of his efforts.

"You had better ring for her," I said to Austin, who was quite near to the bell. "She probably does not know that they have come or that tea is ready."

So Austin rang the bell, and when the maid appeared I told her to find out if Miss Reynard was in the house and if so to let her know that Mr. and Mrs. Dagenham had come.

Apparently she was successful in her quest, for after a few minutes Eve came down, not looking pale as one might reasonably have expected but with heightened colour and shining eyes. I was dumb-foundered at the sight. So this was the effect of knowing that Austin's whole heart and soul were hers; even the tragedy and hopelessness of their situation had not been able to dim the glory of the truth, for the time at least. And I more than ever realised the folly of a woman trying to keep fast hold of the husk when the kernel was gone elsewhere.

I had no opportunity of saying anything to Austin until after Mother and the Colonel had come home and had engrossed Madge's attention. "Come out into the garden. I want to tell you something," I said to him.

He turned towards the wide open window at once and we walked out into the radiance of the fair June sunset together. I caught just a flash of Eve's eyes as we went . . . Poor Eve, it must have been hard for her and she did not know how soon joy was coming.

There was a long walk through a shrubbery at the Warren, from which, indeed, the place was named. Austin and I went along this walk slowly and in silence, I feeling half shy concerning what I had to say to him; and he—well, I cannot be supposed to know what he was thinking of but I should say of his stolen moment of love with Eve. The sun was glinting through the tall trees and shrubs and making strange weird shadows athwart the path which we were treading . . . "I wanted to say something to you, Austin," I began at last, in a sort of desperation.

Austin turned and looked at me. "Why, my dear," he said, just in the same considerate kind voice as of old, "what is wrong?"

"Well, so far as I can see," I replied, "everything is wrong, everything."

"As how?" he asked, his face paling a little.

"Dear Austin," I said slipping my hand into his, "it is no use beating about the bush any longer—I know all."

He fairly staggered in the intensity of his surprise.

"My God!" he muttered under his breath. "How? Tell me, whom have you seen, what have you heard? All, what do you mean?"

Mean . . . Why, that I was in the garden this afternoon when you and Eve thought you were alone with each other," I returned simply. "I heard most of what you said—I felt that I had a right to listen, that it concerned me as much as you two."

"Nancy!" he exclaimed hoarsely, "you don't mean that you—that you———"

"That I know that you and Eve love each other?" I ended. "Yes, I mean just that, of course. What else should I mean?"

He stopped short. "Nancy, I know that I have been a brute—no words of mine can ever express how bitterly sorry I am for all this. I did not mean, that is, I had no idea—and—and——"

"I did not bring you out here to reproach you, Austin," I said with dignity. "Of course I know that you could not either of you help it. You thought you were in love with me, and Heaven knows I thought I was in love with you; but it seems that we were both mistaken and it is much better to find it out now than if we had got married and had found it out afterwards. As it is, there is no reason why you should not marry Eve, just as well as you could have married me."

He turned round. "Nancy, you do allow this? Nancy, I feel dazed—dazed. Am I dreaming, or did you really say that?"

"Oh, I said it right enough," I replied, trying to smile in a whole-hearted way, which I was very far from feeling. "You want to marry her, don't you?"

"Oh, Nancy!" he repeated again.

"Yes, I see that you do. Well, it is quite simple. I will give you to Eve."

"But there is so much to be thought of," he protested. "Your father and mother. . . . what in the world will they say? Eve, will she—will she be inclined to let you make this—this—"

"Sacrifice?" I suggested.

He reddened at the word. "Well, yes, I know it must seem a most conceited thing to say, but I don't mean it in that light at all," he said, with a small show of awkwardness. "But, you see, Nancy, up to this moment I have believed that you were very much in love with me—"

"And now that you find that I am not, that I have been mistaken just as you have been, you are not half as grateful as you might be," I retorted. "Well, this is an ungrateful world, no mistake about it. Austin, am I to tell you in plainer words that I would like to be free of my engagement to you?"

He caught hold of my hands. "Nancy, you are quite sure?" he asked. "And you are not doing this out of a feeling of—of——"

"I am quite quite sure," I replied firmly, "that I would not marry you now for any consideration on earth, not if there was not another man in all the world, not if you begged and prayed me—which I am sure I devoutly hope you won't do—for a year. So don't argue about it any more but accept the gifts the gods offer with thankfulness and with gratitude."

"But your father——"

"Oh, I will explain matters to him, if you like," I said half recklessly, for I felt if I was in for a pennyworth of explanations, I might as well be in for a pound of them.

"You would do that too?" he ejaculated.

"Shall I send Eve out to you?" I asked, for I was beginning to feel that I had had about enough of this sort of thing—for, you know, I really did care, though I made believe so valiantly that I did not.

He was still holding my hands and he looked down at me with a curious expression which I did not understand. "My little Nancy, you have broken me down completely," he said. "What am I to say? How am I to thank you? I can only say that in no sense am I worthy to tie your shoe, if you knew everything; and before you say any thing to Eve I feel I ought to make a confession to you——"

"Not to me," I cried, wrenching my hands away from him. "On no account, if you please. I could imagine nothing more dreadful. If you have anything to say, you can say it to Eve. As for me I have done with you. You know you cannot be on the same terms with both of us. It must be one or the other, and as I have definitely given you up, I cannot be the one. It is not a question which admits of further argument. Now, I am going in. You have just time to tell Eve the decision we have come to before you must think of getting ready for dinner. Let me go now."

But he caught me back again. "But you'll kiss me for the last time, Nancy?"

"No, neither for the first or the last time. You and I have done with each other so far as that sort of thing goes," I replied firmly. And then I turned away and went back towards the house alone.

As I went I looked back over my shoulder and called out to him. "Stay there and I will send her to you."

So I went towards the house, but as I reached the terrace which ran in front of the drawing-room Windows, I met Eve, still looking very white and drawn evidently coming in quest of us.

"Mother wants you for a few minutes," she said as we met.

"I was just coming in," I replied. "I wish you would go down to the warren and tell Austin that I am not coming out again."

"I will," she replied simply,

I stood to watch her go and with a smile turned and went into the house. I found Mother and Madge in the drawing-room. "You wanted me, dear?" I said to her.

"Yes, here is a note from Mrs. Newcombe which I cannot answer until you have seen it. You see, she asks you particularly to this dinner and the servant is waiting for a reply. Will you be back from Dagenham by that time?"

"My dear Mother," I said, taking her hand and speaking in what I felt to be an admirably indifferent voice. "I am going to take your breath away. I cannot go to this party of Mrs. Newcombe's, for the very good reason that I shall be at Dagenham for much longer than a week—unless Madge proves hard-hearted and won't have me there, in which case I shall have gone on some other visit. Austin and I have agreed that, sweet and lovely as we both are, we are not for each other and we have parted."

"You and Austin have quarrelled?" she cried, while Madge echoed the words in the same breath.

"Certainly not," I returned sharply. "We have not had a single word of difference, ever. No, the truth is Austin and I do not care for each other except in a very lukewarm kind of way, and—and—he and Eve have found out that they do."

My Mother stood up in her surprise. "Do you mean to tell me that Austin has deserted you for Eve, and that Eve has stolen your lover away from you?" she cried in a tone of extremest disgust.

"No such thing," I declared firmly. "They have both been self sacrificing and most honourable over the whole affair. As it was, I only found it out by a pure accident. You know, dear Mother, these things are not always within our own control and may happen to any one. And it is all definitely settled, so far as I am concerned, and there is nothing more to say. I think it a perfect mercy that we have found it out before it was too late to remedy the mistake."

"And you don't care?" she cried.

"I don't think that I have ever really been desperately in love with Austin, as one ought to be, you know," I replied, for I felt that I must make my case good or else that I should have put myself on one side for nothing. "And, Mother, Eve is breaking her heart about him. You know what a self-contained girl she has always been and how deeply she feels everything. You must remember how she grieved for our dear old Tom and how we were afraid . . . But you know all that. Well, dear, I don't in the least mind her having won Austin's love, but I do want them both to be happy."

"I don't know **what** your father will say," Mother said at last—and then I kissed her, for I knew that I had won the day.

"Never mind what the Colonel says, dear," I replied. "You know that you can make him see anything in the light in which you wish him to see it. And may I remind you that Mrs. Newcombe's servant is waiting for an answer to her invitation? Madge, I suppose I may count on you to provide me with a haven into which I can hie me to hide my forlorn condition?"

"Oh, Nancy, darling, for a year if you like," she answered stretching out her hand to me. "And Nancy, I must say I do think you the most generous girl I have ever known in all my life. I think Austin a perfect fool to lose the chance of such a wife, yes, I do indeed. And I only hope, darling, that it may be made up to you a thousand times, and that those two will never suffer for what they have done to-day. I only hope that."

"I don't see why they should suffer," I replied, in an undertone, for Mother had gone to her writing-table and was scribbling her note to Mrs. Newcombe. "Poor souls, they have suffered enough as it is."

"I don't know," said Madge, a little curtly, "I have not kept my eyes shut these last few weeks, though I felt it was no good my saying anything about it."

"Well, a case of real desperate love is a very serious thing for the family in which it happens," I remarked, in a joking tone. "And I advise you to hold your peace about this particular instance. You will find it the easiest in the long run. And now, I am going to get dressed for dinner. I suppose I shall have ever such a fuss with the Colonel presently."

"Oh, Mother will have broken the ice for you," said Madge, as I went out of the room.

When I found myself alone in my own room, I turned the key in both the doors, one of which led to the landing and the other into Eve's bedroom. I wanted to have a little while quite to myself to think over the thing which I had done, more or less on the impulse of the moment. Of course, it was too late to undo it, yet I wanted to think of it all the same.

Well, I had done it. Austin and I were nothing to each other now and never would be anything to each other again. Did I care so much? Well, yes, to be quite honest, I think I did, nay, I know that I did.

Still, even in my pain, the pain of being slighted, I still felt that I had chosen the better part and that, by and by, I should have my reward, and even if I never had that, yet at the very worst I should in the course I had taken find the lesser pain.

And I was still sitting in front of my dressing-table staring abstractedly at my-self in the glass, when I heard the door which led into Eve's room gently tried. Then Eve's voice came to me . . . "Nancy, Nancy, open the door, I want to speak to you."

CHAPTER XXII.
A FACE I KNEW!

Their hearts may be fountains whose eyes are flint, and may inwardly bleed who do not outwardly weep. —FULLER.

In the soul Possess a secret, silent dwelling-place, Where with a silent vis-age memory sits. —TENNYSON.

AS I expected, the Colonel did not take the new state of things quite so easily as our mother had done. I saw when we sat down to dinner that evening that he had as yet, heard nothing. He chaffed me about my forlorn state to the great discomfiture of both Eve and Austin, and then he drank to our next merry meeting, for, as he said, he did not count the parting breakfast which we should partake of together as being of any importance. As each sally was flung forth so did Austin look more un-comfortable and Eve more wretched. But the Colonel never noticed that anything out of the common had transpired and joked cheerily on until the meal at last came to an end.

I had given Austin and Geoffrey a hint to betake themselves away as soon as possible after dinner, and as soon as I knew that the coast was clear, I went in and sat down at the table with my father, who was enjoying a last glass of some thin Rhenish wine and smoking an after dinner cigarette. "Hollo, is it you?" he remarked, as I appeared. "Why, child, you are getting near to the period of feeling like 'Leah, the Forsaken.' "

"And a good deal more like it than you think," I returned promptly.

He looked up.

"Hey, what d'you mean?" he demanded a little sharply.

"My dear old Daddy," I replied, "I want you to prepare yourself for a tremendous surprise. I am not going to be married after all. You were quite right—I did not know my own mind. I do know it now and I am minded to stay at home a little longer with you and Mother."

My father turned and stared at me.

"What!" he almost shouted. "Is it that you have chucked Austin—"

"Well, you needn't put it in that horrid way," I said meekly. "I haven't exactly done that, as a matter of fact. No, but I have had my doubts as to the depth of our feelings for some little time, and—and—and this is the surprise, Daddy—I find that Austin and Eve——"

"WHAT!" he bawled out, suddenly growing scarlet with indignation. "Do you mean to tell me that Eve, that a daughter of mine——"

"Now, now," I put in soothingly. "Don't excite yourself over it, dear. They have both behaved beautifully and with ever consideration towards me, and all you are wanted to do is to bless them and let them get married quietly and go away and enjoy their happiness." And then I gave him the outline of the story, just as I had done to Mother.

I am bound to admit that at first I thought he meant to hold out against them for ever. He stormed and raved and blustered and finally but this question to me, which much as I wished to make the path of the lovers smooth and easy for them, I must admit was a regular clincher. "Tell me," He thundered. "If Gray is able to change his mind so easily as this between you two, how am I to know that he will not change it again when some other fancy strikes him? Answer me that."

I could no answer it for a moment. "Dear Daddy," I said at last, "you cannot have forgotten what trouble Madge Used to give you on this very matter. How many times was she engaged? Well, you never made half as much fuss then as you are doing now. I don't think it's quite fair, do your?"

"Would you like me to be pleased with this fellow for jilting you," he cried, "and to be pleased with Eve for taking your lover away from you?"

"But she has done so, and he has not done so. I tell you I found it out by a mere accidents Neither of them were at all willing to take the smallest advantage over me. They cannot help their feelings—poor things, they are miserable enough over it."

"And serve 'em right too," growled the Colonel testily. "I've no patience with feelings like those. Ugh! You make me ill when you make excuses for them."

"But you'll be nice and kind and sweet to them—to please me, won't you, dear old Daddy?" I put in persuasively.

"H'm, that's the way dear old Daddy is to be managed, is it?" he returned. He was still vexed, but I felt that he was relenting.

"They don't want a very long engagement," I remarked, though neither of them had so much as hinted at the subject to me. "You see, Eve is not as young as I and there is not the same need for her waiting. I think," I added artfully, "that was one of the reasons why you insisted on my waiting at least a year, that I might have plenty of time for changing my mind."

"Go away, you saucy young baggage," said the Colonel, bursting out laughing in spite of himself.

"Then I may tell them that they have nothing to fear from you?" I remarked.

"You can tell them that I shall only consent because *you* have asked it," he replied brusquely. "Eve knows what the fellow is and has had a pretty sample of his constancy. She goes into it with her eyes wide open and cannot, and indeed never must, blame me if the marriage turns out a most dismal failure. Still, Nancy, my dear little girl, I should like you to satisfy me on one point. Are you quite sure that this business is not hurting you very much? Are you sure you are not doing all this out of a mere Quixotic sense of chivalry?"

I slipped my arm round my father's neck. "Dear Daddy," I said, "I don't think I was really in love with Austin. Sometimes, do you know I used to stick fast when I was talking to him because I could not think of anything to say. Surely, there must have been something wanting; everything could not have been as it should have been. Did you ever find yourself stuck fast for want of something to say when you were engaged to Mother?"

"Never!" declared my father, with emphasis.

"And even if I were still a little fond of him, don't you think it is better to part than to go on, knowing that there was another between us? Why, Daddy, I would not put myself into such a wretched condition for all the world!"

"And you are right, my darling," he cried in his tenderest accents. "It *is* better to find such mistakes out before rather than after. But I don't feel so sure that there is any great chance of happiness for Eve, and I don't know that she deserves it."

"Poor Eve! Don't say that to her, dear," I implored. "For she is feeling just the same herself."

So it was all right. I went and told them that the way was fairly smooth, and then I sought out Madge and arranged that I should go back to Dagenham with her the following day. And then I pleaded weariness and went off to bed, and, if I tell the truth, I must confess that I cried myself to sleep.

I woke up about six o'clock in the morning and lay thinking over the strange changes which had taken place in my life during the past few hours. Well, it was all for the best no doubt, but—but—it did hurt, oh, yes, it did hurt, and I knew that, all my stout protestations to the contrary, I did love Austin still.

However, it was no use thinking of that now. I had done the deed and there could be no going back therefrom. To one thing I had quite made up my mind, that cost me what it might, I would never let any one of my people know how much it had been to me to give up my lover—my lover, did I say? I meant rather my fiancé!

I rose at the usual time and went to breakfast with as bright a morning face as I could muster up at such short notice. Once or twice I saw Eve looking at me in wonder, evidently thoroughly astonished at my cold-bloodedness in being able to appear after such a loss as Austin. Really, I found myself several times on the verge of laughing out aloud, the expression on her face was so comical to me.

The Colonel was what old Nurse would have described as "chuffy!" That is to say, he was just as cross as two sticks and kept flinging curt remarks down for anyone to take up and challenge if they chose. And as the desire of every one of us was to avoid anything approaching to a quarrel, nobody did take them up and a series of uncomfortable silences was the result. A more uncomfortable meal I never sat through.

Immediately after it was over I went off to Dagenham with Madge and Geoffrey. And right glad I was to get away. Madge and Geoffrey too were perfectly jubilant, and did not hesitate to say that they would not have remained another day at the Warren for any consideration whatever.

"When one thinks of the settlements to be talked over, and the details of the wedding and the trousseau, and Father's thundery looks and dear Mother's sighs, I must say that I think Eve is getting her sweetheart at a very dear price. I am sure it would have been much better for him to have gone off to London and have let Father get a bit used to the new state of things rather than staying on to bear the brunt of it all. However, it is their look-out, and we need not trouble *our* heads about them." This was what Madge said, and really Madge had had so many love-affairs and broken engagements in *her* time that I regarded her as an authority.

A week went by and we saw nothing of the lovers. Mother and the Colonel came over to lunch one day, but Father never mentioned them and Mother would not say anything of how they had been getting on. I learned that Austin had left the Warren the same day as we did and that he had since been staying at the "Rose and Crown," which was the principal hotel in Minchester. "I believe they are going to be married in about six weeks' time," Mother let slip very unwillingly.

She had however, brought a little note from Eve to Madge, which Madge passed on to me. This was what it said:

"DEAREST MADGE,

"If you think it would not be disagreeable to Nancy, Austin and I would like to come over to lunch one day this week that we may tell you our plans. If you think dear Nancy would mind it in the very least, of course we would not dream of coming. You might let me have a word to say how she is. Everything is pretty miserable here, the Colonel black as a thunder-cloud, and Mother as cold as ice and as close as wax. Everybody asking questions and throwing out hints, and so we feel that the sooner we hurry things on and get out of it the better. It does seem so queer, when Nancy has been such an angel to us both, that everyone else should be doing their best to make us miserable. Even Nurse shakes her head every time she sees me and after pointed remarks about her dear lamb at Dagenham, goes off with a sort of stifled prayer that it may all turn out for the best. She generally adds that it is very doubtful, which is re-assuring to say the least of it. Let me hear when we may come, if at all.

"Always your aff. sister,

"EVE."

Madge looked at me rather doubtfully, and I answered the thought which I knew was in her mind. "My dear, pray let the poor souls come. I don't bear them any ill-will, I assure you. They could not help it and I think it is rather cruel of everyone to be making them feel it so. Let them come whenever you and they like."

Madge therefore wrote to that effect and sure enough the very next day, over they came, coming in a hired conveyance from the "Rose and Crown." I did think it was mean of Father not to have lent them the pony-trap at least, but I could not help laughing outright as they drove up. "Is this what you call semi- state?" I asked derisively as they drew up at the entrance.

Poor Eve began to cry when she got into the morning-room. "Oh, Nannie darling, if you knew what I have gone through!" she sobbed as I kissed her.

I put my arms about her. "Never mind, dear, it will soon be over," I whispered, "and the afterward will be worth it. You can go away for a good long tour and when you come back again, they will have forgotten all about it. And perhaps, who knows, I may be married too. So don't fret, dear."

She rested her head against me and dried her eyes. "Oh, Nannie, Nannie, how could you give him up?" she sighed.

I laughed outright. "What, is it so bad as that?" I asked. "Why, I don't mind telling you now that I did feel a bit bad over it the first two days or so; but I have never felt and never could feel like that. Anyway, it's lucky for you that I do feel as I do, isn't it?"

And I was perfectly honest in what I said. As soon as I saw the two together and perceived what an overwhelming love Eve's was for him, I knew that mine had not been the real thing at all, but only the outcome of propinquity and circumstance. From that moment I never grudged my sister her great happiness and I tried to show them so in every way I possibly could.

"My dear, it must be perfectly wretched for you," cried Madge, who was the most easy-going creature in existence and hated quarrels and scenes of every shape and kind.

"Oh, it's horrid. You would never believe it was the dear old Warren," answered Eve, with the tears coming into her eyes again. "Even to-day when Mother knew we were coming over here, she said that it was positively indecent to be coming flaunting my happiness in Nancy's face. And such a way of putting it, don't you know. I told Mother that when Nancy had done so much for us, the very least we could do was to let her know our plans, but she only shut her lips in that severe way of hers—you know—and put up her head, as if—as if I was telling a lie about it. Oh, I am most miserable, except for that one thing."

"My dear girl," I remarked, "you may make your mind quite easy about me. I am not pining, am I, Madge?"

"Not the very least little bit," returned Madge promptly. "I wonder if you would like to come over here for a week or so——"and there she broke off short and looked doubtfully at me as if to ask me to endorse the invitation.

"Yes, do come; it will be ever so much nicer," I said instantly. "At all events, you will have peace and quietness here with no one to bully you for being happy. Pray don't let any idea of me keep you away."

So they arranged it should be done, and indeed the very next day the poor fugitives came out with a modest amount of luggage and left the storm and thunder-clouds behind for a little time.

I went in to Minchester the following day to see Mother and to assure her that she and the Colonel need have no fear or anxiety about me. I think she was more satisfied when she had seen me and had talked it all over again, and she even went so far as to promise that she would reproach Eve no more, and she would try to take Austin back into his old place in her esteem. And when I went back to Dagenham I carried the good news with me to the no small relief of those mostly concerned.

Mother had suggested my returning home and leaving them with Madge and Geoffrey, but this I preferred not to do. "No, dear," I said, "if I do that, it will give rise to no end of complications and rumours. People will think that I have fled to be out of their way, whereas I don't mind them the least little bit."

So I went back and peace reigned once more. The weather was simply lovely and we almost lived out of doors. Indeed we regularly had breakfast and tea out of doors and greatly enjoyed the plan. People came and went and we used to hustle the lovers out of the way of those that were likely to be too inquisitive, and we shut up any hints regarding them with the most ruthless bluntness. So the blazing summer days went by, each one bringing the two nearer to their freedom from vexation and worry. And every day any lingering pains I might have had drooped and died and I ceased to feel any regret for the lover who was mine no longer.

And then something happened, something awful, terrible, in fact the most awful and terrible thing which could by any chance possibly have happened to me. I began to see again!

It came out of something that Madge was saying one glorious afternoon when we were sitting in the garden. "I cannot think how it was," she was saying, "that you did not know that Austin was getting to care for Eve—I mean, I wonder you did not know it as you know other things."

"But no clairvoyante can see for herself," I replied.

"Is that really so?" she exclaimed in great surprise.

I told her then all about Miss Lorenzi and what she had said on the subject, and while I was still speaking someone came out of the house and fetched my sister indoors for some purpose or other. She got up and went away saying that she would be back presently, and I sat still in the big wicker chair thinking how lovely the view was and of how Miss Lorenzi had told Austin's thoughts that day at Milan.

And while I was sitting there alone, I became aware that I was going to see something. The symptoms, you know, were always just the same, my head began to turn slowly round and a thick white mist to come in front of my eyes.

Why, it was an old vision, one which I had seen before, which was slowly forming itself before me. Yes, I had seen the bare, ill-furnished room before, not a doubt of it. Yes, it was a presentment of Mr. Warrender's quarters in Danford Barracks, just as I had seen it that night at the Warren when we were all sitting round the table playing the game of Consequences! Yes, it was the same room, and I saw Edward Warrender come in and fill his pipe and drag himself wearily away; then the red-haired soldier servant who tidied up the place and, after filling his pipe, went out also, shutting the door behind him. And then the room was empty for a little while, and after a minute or so, the door was cautiously opened and I saw a face I knew look in, as if to see if anyone was there. A face I knew did I say? A face I knew—the face I knew better than all others, the face of Austin Gray!

CHAPTER XXIII.
AN OLD VISION!

None are evil wholly, OP evil all at once. —DR. W. SMITH.

To thine own self be true, And it most follow, as the night the day, Thou canst not then be false to any man. —*Hamlet.*

THE scene was not new to me, I had seen it all before, only the one fact of present importance—the personality of the man—had entirely and completely slipped my memory. I went through the whole of the picture again, just as I had done that night when we all sat round the table laughing and joking over the game of Consequences. I saw the man in uniform looking about the room and reading the letters, and then I saw him take out a bunch of keys and try the drawer in which the star was. I saw him take out the star, burn the case, and try to push out the stones as he stood on the hearth-rug. Yes, I saw it all and the man was Austin, Austin, Austin, whom I liked so well and who was going to marry my sister, my dear sister, in less than a month's time from now!

When I came to myself again, I was still alone, Heaven be thanked for that, lying back in the big basket chair and trembling in every limb as though an ague had seized me. Enough, too, to make me shiver and shake! I tried to think, to decide what to do for the best—whether to disclose everything to Eve, whether to take Madge into my confidence, whether to tax Austin himself with the truth and leave to him the task of breaking off the engagement, making what excuse he would and leaving Eve in merciful ignorance of the real pause. All these thoughts raced through my mind with the rapidity of lightning, yet I could not decide which would be the best for me to do. I almost thought that the kindest thing to do would be to tell Austin that everything had revealed itself to me. Of course, this would let him off the easiest of all, and yet, I was in doubt whether my poor sister would not suffer more if I took this course than if I told her the truth. After all, why should I think of him? He had not thought of us, for he must have known that my father, had he been aware of his connection with the diamond star incident, would have immediately put the very strongest veto on even a slight acquaintance, to say nothing of a closer tie.

I was still in the same quandary when Madge came back again, and then the footman came out with the tea which he set before her on a many-tiered table which comfortably held both the tray and the different plates of cake and bread and butter which constituted the meal.

"I don't know where the others are," she said cheerfully, as she began to pour out the tea. "Geoffrey won't be home, of course; he has gone to look at a roof some miles away. He is sure to get tea there and have a little gossip with Mrs. Jones, who loves him dearly and always has quite a spread in his honour. I have not the least idea where *they* can be." She laughed softly as she spoke; we always spoke of Eve and Austin as *they.*

I took my tea from Madge, but did not hazard any suggestion as to the whereabouts of the lovers. In truth, I was not at all keen on seeing either of them and, indeed, if anyone had come suddenly in and had told us that Austin had met with an accident and had broken his neck I should have been inclined to hail the news as the most merciful thing that had happened for many and many a day.

"Have some cake," said Madge. "It is extra good to-day."

She passed the plate of hot tea-cake and I helped myself, more to avoid comment than because I really wanted to eat anything. I did not, however, escape notice, as I was anxious to do. Madge looked at me sharply once or twice, on which I tried hard to conjure up a smile and an indifferent remark about something, anything, in which I succeeded very badly. "Nance, you have been seeing things again, haven't you?" she asked.

I looked at her. I tried my best to tell a lie and say no, but the words stuck in my throat and refused to slip off the end of my tongue. "Don't ask me about it, Madge, and pray don't say anything about it to Mother or the others. I—I—have seen a vision that came to me before."

"You don't mean it! Which one?" she asked eagerly.

I could not help answering. "The one where the star was stolen," I replied faintly. I wonder that my face did not betray me and that she did not see in a moment what was in my mind.

"How very strange," Madge exclaimed. "I wonder why that, of all others, should have come back to you? However, thank Goodness that it was nothing new, that it was not some fresh misfortune."

It was on the tip of my tongue to say that a fresh misfortune had come upon us, when a new thought flashed suddenly into my mind. What if I parted them and any one supposed that I had done it from sheer spite at Eve's having taken my lover away from me! I had no proof of the truth of what my strange power showed me, no real proof. How was I to be quite quite sure that it really was Austin who took the star? I might be sure in my own mind and, after all, it might turn out that he had never been in the 26th, and that for once I had been deceived. If that should happen, how should I be able to make people believe that I had acted from the most conscientious motives? I simply could never do it.

Besides, I was not sure; my gift might have played me false. I had had Austin so much on my mind of late that he might have got mixed up in my mind with old impressions, and so have worked himself into that particular picture. Could I, dare I brand a man for ever and ruin my sister's whole chance of happiness by making such a disclosure as this? No, I felt with all my soul that I must keep silence at least for a time, at least until some other confirmation of my suspicions came to me.

We were still sitting there when the two came through the little wicket-gate from the village. I had just time to say to Madge—"Don't say anything about that," when they reached us.

"Is tea over?" Eve asked ever so gaily.

"Not at all; Nance and I have only just begun," Madge replied. She had a wonderful arrangement for keeping water boiling, a sort of a spirit lamp which stood in a smart brass coal-pan, on which she set the kettle over a little open-work brass stand. As she spoke, she filled up the tea-pot and began to pour the tea out. "And where have you been, good people?" she asked.

"Down to the village to get some sweets," replied Eve, who was famous in our family for a love of sugar-plums.

"But not beyond anything so homely as tea, I hope," laughed Madge.

"By no means; on the contrary, I am ready for an enormous feed," Eve declared.

They both seemed in the very best of spirits, indeed it would be hard to say whether Eve or Austin was the gayer of the two. Eve displayed her sweets and divided them put among us, and Austin declared that Dagenham was so cheap, judging by the price of lollipops, that it would be a wise move to take a small house and settle there. Then Madge gave her experiences of the absolute want of cheapness of Dagenham and everything in it, and they talked and chaffed each other finely, while I sat still and silent thinking of what had happened a short time earlier and wondering whether it were true or not. I watched him more closely than I had ever done but I could not tell at all if I were right or wrong, only a sort of painful recognition came to me that this was why I fancied I had seen him before.

I went back over that time, trying to recall his tone and look when I declared that I was sure we had met before, but nothing came to help me in any way. I had only a vivid remembrance of his scoffing air when he declared that he did not believe in anything of the kind, and that his only uncanny superstition was that we had lived many times and that we went up or down in the world according to the way in which we had behaved ourselves in our last phase of life.

Yet, why should that particular dream or mental picture have come back to me? I had not thought of it for ages, there had been nothing which need in any way have recalled it to me, and moreover, it seemed as fresh to me as on the day on which it happened. Was it, or was it not, true? Had he, or had he not, done it? These two questions put themselves to me over and over again, in fifty different forms at least. And at the end I was just as puzzled and just as uncertain as I had been in the beginning.

At last, Eve noticed that I was unusually quiet. I fancy that she had always a lingering fear that I was breaking my heart, and every now and then felt qualms of conscience on my account. So she was always the one to notice if anything went at all wrong with me, and she noticed my silence then, "You are very quiet, Nancy," she said, looking at me a little anxiously.

"A bit of a headache," I replied, with what I knew must be an admirable carelessness. "Nothing for you to worry about." Well, to be candid, that was neither more nor less than a downright lie, but I felt that it was a forgivable one, for, after all, why should I harry her with what was on my mind? It was no fault of hers, even if the very worst proved to be true.

"The sun has been so hot to-day," she said, putting up her hand and smoothing back her own heavy hair, which hung thickly over her forehead. Then changed her tone . . . "Have a sweetie, they are really not half bad for a village shop. Try a bit of this nougât! Really, I could scarcely believe my eyes when I saw it glorifying the little counter."

I did try a piece of the nougât, for it was a confection of which I was known to be fond and my refusal would only have excited further comment. It was good nougât too, very good, and I congratulated Eve on her find. Then they went on talking and making fun and I slipped back into my quietude without exciting any more remarks, for which I was thankful. So we dawdled through that lovely summer afternoon, and presently the nurse brought out the little heir, who came and toddled to and fro as fine and bright a little fellow as any mother was ever proud of. He too had his share of the nougât and other sweets, perhaps rather more than his share, but then, as Eve said, who could resist him? Certainly, none of us.

While young Reggie was with us he found his way to Austin's side and clambered on to his knee where he sat playing peep-bo with me. You see, I was sitting next to Austin and so the child was between us. The effect of this was like magic, for I suddenly became aware that the little fellow had formed a perfect medium between us and that I could read Austin's thoughts just as I could read a book.

My first impression was one of huge and overwhelming self-reproach, of wave after wave of absolute penitence, flooding his whole nature and filling his heart with alternate grief and gushes of love. This lasted so long that I was dazzled by it, dazzled and confused. I took the child's little; chubby hand in mine and tried with all my might to learn the cause of this strange state of feeling. I had not long to wait. The boy sat quietly munching his bar of nougât and kept as still as if he had known my reason for wishing him to do so. First there came to me the thought that this was the dearest little chap that I had ever seen, that he was Eve's nephew and her favourite among all children. Then that there might one day come to me—to the thinker (that, of course, was Austin, for the thoughts came straight to me as his) just such a dear little child, his and Eve's! The very thought seemed to fill his heart with an overwhelming sense of intense love, and was followed by a feeling of horror that possibly some day, an enemy might desire to harm the child, as one had desired to harm this child, not of ill-will towards the child himself, but out of enmity to his parents.

Then through that dear little innocent child came as clear to my mind as a painted picture the unravelling of the mystery of Joan Manning. Good heavens, I tell you I don't know how I sat there, calmly and outwardly in peace with all men, and saw all that came to my over-wrought brain that day. But I did it; I had a purpose to win, an end to gain, and I did it somehow or other.

First there came back to me that scene in which Joan Manning's real position had been revealed to me. I learned more about her now than I had gathered then, for I knew in a moment through the strange mediumship of Austin and the child, that she had been on terms of the most complete intimacy with my sister's lover, and that it was through him and at his instigation that she had entered my sister's service and had tried to poison her child!

With what horror I received all these impressions I can hardly describe. I managed to keep my head so that I did not let the others know what was going on, and I clutched hold of Reggie with a despairing grip so as to miss nothing of what was in Austin Gray's soul. I pitied him, oh, yes, yes, with all my heart. That was the burden of his thoughts, wave after wave of absolute penitence, mingled with devoutest pæans of thankfulness that the plot had been discovered in time. And for Joan Manning no more than an overwhelming horror, as for some devil that would drag him down to everlasting hell! What thoughts, what anguish, what regret, and hovering over all, his intense love for Eve, a love that was as a religion, a creed, an eternity!

The child struggled down from off his knee and the visions vanished in a moment. I looked at Austin and asked myself whether he was as I had gathered from my impressions of his thoughts—whether all this was but the imaginings of an over-wrought brain, the mere outcome of a fevered fancy, or whether it was all true? I watched him narrowly as he sat beside me in a huge basket chair, his feet stretched out in front of him and a cigarette between his lips. Yes, it was true enough! I saw that the cigarette had gone out, though he had not smoked more than a third of it, and his thoughts were evidently very far away. In my anxiety I put out my hand and quietly laid it on his. "A penny for your thoughts, Austin," I said, in as light a tone as I could assume.

He started as if he had been shot and shook my hand off, decidedly, sitting up straight in his chair and shaking himself together in a resolute way, which quite prevented my touching him again. "I beg your pardon . . . I was very rude. In truth, my thoughts were very far away at that moment. Forgive me, it was quite unpardonable."

He put the cigarette between his lips again and tried to smoke again. . . "It has gone out," I said quietly.

He threw it away and then he turned and looked at me.

"What is it, Nancy?" he said.

"What is what?" I returned, evading the implied question.

"Why did you want to know what I was thinking of?" he asked, in an undertone, for the others were gaily laughing over some antics of the child's.

"You looked as if your thoughts might be interesting," I replied.

"God knows they were not that," he said in a very bitter tone. "At all events, my best wish for you is that you may never have such thoughts. But you never could. It is impossible."

"I sincerely hope so," I said, gravely.

"What do you mean?"

"They were evidently not pleasant," I said, "or you would not have spoken as you did just now."

Madge made a move just then, and I rose at once and followed her into the house. She slipped her hand under my arm as we walked along the broad terrace walk. "My dear child," she said kindly, "I do not know whether you are feeling ill or not, but you look as white as a ghost."

"Oh, my head is all queer to-day," I replied. "Don't worry about me. I shall be all right when I have had a good sleep."

"You don't think there is anything in your seeing that room again?" she asked.

"How anything? What do you mean?"

"Well, one never knows. It seems strange that you should see it at all, after all these years and when there has been nothing in any way to bring it back to mind. I don't understand it all."

"Oh, one cannot account for these things, Madge," I said vehemently. . . "You will never know how I wish with all my heart and soul that I was like other people. I know this power of mine will kill me one of these days. I feel convinced of it. And what is the good of it? If it would warn me, it would then be different. But it only tells me something which nothing can alter. What's the good of it?"

"Well, I don't see how you can say that," Madge replied seriously. "We owe our child's life to it; and there was that affair of the star. We don't know how that might have affected us all if you had not found out who really took it. Think of the man who was accused of it. No, dear, it is a great nuisance to you, but you must not say that there is no good in it, for we have proved that there is Why . . ." with a great shuddering sigh that was half a gasp for breath, "I might have married that . . . other one . . . Oh, Nancy, darling, don't ever say again that there is no good in it. I know that it has made all the difference in my life."

Of course, I could not controvert anything of this, so I parted from my sister with a careless word and went straight to my own roam. And once there, I sat down by the open window and tried to think what I had better do? What could I do? For the life of me I did not know, I could not tell. I had gained enough of his thoughts to know that let his past be what it might, Austin Gray was simply devoted to my sister now and that his whole thoughts were of regret for the villanies he had perpetrated in the past. His whole desires for the future were to make himself more worthy of her, to get closer and closer to her so that her white life might purify his black one. And it was black, the blackest with which I had ever been brought in contact.

I wondered why it had been that he had any desire to do the kind of things of which I knew him to be guilty, for they were for the most part things of which no man brought up in the position of a gentleman is ever suspected? One can understand a man, world-worn and steeped in sin from his cradle upward, taking his neighbours goods, in short being a thief. One can understand a man hungered and homeless, stealing food with which to satisfy his natural cravings or the means with which he may get food. But one cannot understand a man who has large means of his own, yielding to an impulse which will if found out ensure his ruin, and prevent his well-being in this world for ever. And even if, to take the most merciful view, we regarded such a theft as the act of a kleptomaniac, the same excuse did not hold good for those other things that he had done, the poisoning of Madge's little child, well, the ***attempted*** poisoning, I perhaps should rather say, and the leaving of his accomplice in prison while he went off scot-free and was actually on the verge of marriage with another.

As all these thoughts came crowding in upon my brain, I felt that however unpalatable the task would be, I could not, must not hide the truth any longer and I made up my mind that after dinner, I would tell Madge everything. She, I knew would be merciful, and spare me the hideous task of denouncing him, and Geoffrey would go over to the Warren and break the horrid news to my father and mother. But oh, though I had made up my mind, the whole thing was hideous, most hideous, and at that moment I would gladly have run away to the uttermost ends of the earth, so that I might hide myself from everyone I knew for ever.

CHAPTER XXIV.
ONE GOLDEN THREAD OF TRIUMPH !

Love will creep whaur it mauna gang. —*Scottish Proverb.*

Let not him that putteth his hand to the plough look backwards; Though the ploughshare cut through the flowers of life to its fountains, Though it pass o'er the graves of the dead and the hearths of the living. —*Courtship of Miles Standish.*

I WAS late for dinner that evening. I had forgotten until quite the last moment that there were guests to dinner, not exactly a dinner-party, just the Rector and his wife, and a young man owning the place next to Dagenham. The odd thing was that Madge was late also. When I got down into the drawing-room I found the three guests patiently waiting and trying to look as if it were quite the usual thing to reach the drawing-room before the hostess. True, Geoffrey was there and he had evidently apologised duly and truly for he had got his excuses so firmly implanted on his mind that he even made them to me.

"The fact is," he said, "Madge has had an accident. She will be here in a few minutes."

"Is she hurt? What has happened?" I asked in alarm.

"No, no, she is not hurt at all; but the youngster was in our room helping us to dress, and he upset a bottle of hair-oil all down his mother's gown."

"I did not know Madge used hair-oil," I said, feeling greatly relieved that the accident was nothing more serious.

"No more she does; it was brilliantine of mine," Geoffrey admitted. "But, of course, she had to change her frock and, as luck would have it, it was one of those affairs which lace up, and it took as much time undoing as it had taken putting on."

"It was lucky it was nothing worse," I said, sitting down by Mrs. Ladworth. "And, at such times, one's fingers seem to be all thumbs."

"Oh, yes, indeed they do; but there is no need for Mrs. Dagenham to put herself out about it. It won't hurt us to wait ten minutes or so," was the reply of the parson's kind little wife, who was herself a woman who made it one of the first rules of life never to worry about unnecessary things.

"And as nobody else is ready in time to-night, perhaps it is just as well that the hostess should be fate too," I returned smiling.

However, the very next one to appear was Madge herself who came in dressed in a black gown with a good deal of white lace about it and full of pretty apologies. Then Eve followed and finally Austin himself appeared, looking so handsome, so manly, so happy and contented with himself and all the world, that I came to the conclusion that my imagination had been playing me false and that I had been altogether and entirely mistaken in having in any way mixed him up with those old and tragic visions of my past.

Dinner was served immediately and as the table at Dagenham was a round one and our party one of eight, Madge had departed from the conventional pairing off and placing of the diners so that husbands and wives might not sit together. I was sent in with Austin and had the Hector on my other hand, and Eve sat next to Austin on his left hand. For a party of eight it was an admirably arranged table and everybody seemed perfectly satisfied with his or her fate.

For myself, I was glad to be next to Austin, for I knew that I should be sure to have a chance of communicating with his thoughts, and really, his whole appearance had so shaken my belief in what I had found out, that I was more doubtful than ever as to the advisability of saying so much as a single word about him.

We had just got settled in our places when Madge leaned forward and said to me:

"Oh, by the way, Nancy, I've got a piece of news for you. Who do you think has come to Manchester and is coming out here to-morrow morning to see us?"

"How should I know?" I returned, for I never was good at guessing anything.

"Mr. Warrender, Edward Warrender," said Madge. "Mother says he is just the same as he used to be, not altered at all."

"Mr. Warrender!" I echoed.

Involuntarily, I turned to see what effect this piece of news would have upon Austin. And, if I had doubted, for a few minutes, the justice of my suspicions, the accuracy of my strange power, it was surely confirmed in that moment, for his face was the colour of ashes and his hand which was resting on the edge of the table was shaking visibly. In very pity I forbore to look any longer, but turned again to Madge asking when she had heard the news?

"I have just had a letter from Mother. I should have thought that she would have been upset by the seeing him, but apparently she is just as delighted as if one of her own sons had come back again. I am so glad that it is so. He is a dear boy and, you know," she added, turning to Mr. Ladworth, "he was our dear Tom's greatest friend and was with him when he died."

I did not listen to what Mr. Ladworth had to say but sat back in my chair wishing I were in bed, away, anywhere but where I was. I should have to tell all I knew now; if I did not the first time that Austin and Edward Warrender met, everything would of necessity come out. How I wished it might come out without my being mixed up in it!

I scarcely know how it was, but somehow that night I became aware that I could read Austin's thoughts as clearly as I could read a book and without any medium or contact. I had the merciful shield of a headache, so that I could sit back in my chair and let the tide of food and conversation go on without me. And as I sat there, I knew just what was passing in the mind of the man beside me. What tumult of thoughts, of hopes, fears, regrets, and through all just one golden thread of triumph—I suppose at having won Eve's love.

And I was sorry for him too. He did not know the Colonel as we did, or surely there would be no thread of triumph in that conflicting chaos of ideas! Yes, I was sorry for him, and yet for all our sakes I was glad that Edward Warrender had arrived before it was too late, before he and Eve had become one.

I scarcely know how I got through that dinner. Once or twice Madge asked me in an undertone if my head was very bad, and once if I would like to go away from the table. "Not at all," I replied, "my head is not aching so very much now. I would much rather stay, though I don't care to talk much."

Yes, I wanted to stay that I might know still further the workings of Austin

Gray's mind, and that I might satisfy myself that he would not stay to meet Edward Warrender face to face. He only spoke to me once or twice during the whole of the meal, but he talked in a very low voice to Eve and though I tried to hear the subject of their conversation, I did not succeed in doing so. I half fancied that he had an idea of leaving Dagenham early in the morning and that he would persuade Eve to go with him or to join him later on. And in order to prevent her from doing that I fully made up my mind that I would tell her everything, even to the fact of his having instigated that woman to make away with Madge's little child.

I was just thinking this when an awful thought came into my mind, came like a flash of light; ***that was not Austin Gray's only villainy!*** What about that affair when Tom was nearly stabbed to death by a native, who was killed by his dog? Surely, he was at the bottom of that also. The very idea served almost to petrify me. I shrank away from him as if he might suddenly turn and kill me without word or warning.

But the next minute, the impression came to me that Austin had no such thought in his mind, no such desire in his heart, it was a crushed and stricken man who sat beside me, and if he could have undone all the black and horrid past, he would have done it at any price. If he could have started straight and clean, with such a father and mother as we had had, if he could have had an Eve from the beginning, he would perhaps never have known those wild desires for revenge, that black longing to crush his enemies under his feet that had so influenced his life afterward. At least I know that this was the way in which he put it to himself, as he sat beside me turning over in his mind all that had happened in the past and all that was likely to happen in the future. And through all there ran that one golden thread of triumph!

By the time the meal was over and we four ladies were free to go into the cool drawing-room, I was feeling perfectly exhausted and nerve-spent. You see, during the past few hours I had passed through a sort of mental furnace and, so far from having come out of the fire softened and chastened, I was only conscious of a general feeling of having been bruised and beaten.

Madge touched my hand as I passed by on my way to the long French window opening on to the terrace. "I believe your head has been dreadful, dear," she said pitifully.

"Oh, no, it is not my head especially," I replied. "I am going outside to get a breath of air this hot night."

"It is hot. Mrs. Ladworth, would you like to go on the terrace?"

"I think it would be rather nice," said she.

"Then let us go out. We will have our coffee out there," said Madge, who loved to be out of doors and as we used to tell her would like to sleep on the terrace if such a habit were feasible.

Accordingly, we all trooped out, well I might as well have said that the four of us did so. We were soon joined by the men, who declared that it was too hot for them to care for cigarettes or wine. They did not find it too hot for coffee, and very soon we found it so much too cool that we were glad to go in again and seek the shelter of the house.

Usually, little dinner parties in the country are kept up rather late, but it happened that Mr. and Mrs. Ladworth were going off on their summer holiday, which they meant to spend in Switzerland, and were starting from Dagenham at six o'clock in the morning. They naturally wanted to get to bed in tolerably good time and so left very soon after we went indoors. Mr. Vane, however, remained on and Geoffrey proposed a game of "Poker" by way of enlivening ourselves. I think we were all glad enough and we sat down at once, and Geoffrey began the work of portioning out the counters. Mr. Vane came and sat by me and asked me if I would go partners with him which I declined to do, having always magic luck at cards and therefore never being keen on sharing it with any one else. He went partners with Madge instead, Geoffrey played for himself and Eve went in with Austin. We began with a jack-pot and had got as far as "Aces or better," when there was a sound of wheels along the drive which made Geoffrey look up at Mr. Vane.

"Is that your trap, Vane?" he asked. "Why did you not put up here?"

"I did," said he. "It is not mine. I don't let my fellow drive at that pace."

Geoffrey went on dealing and for a moment we thought no more of the trap on the drive. Then there was the sound of voices in the hall and the next moment my father, followed by Edward War-render, strode into the room.

"I must apologize for disturbing you at this unseemly hour, Geoffrey," he said brusquely. "But information so important has come to me this evening that I could not wait until morning to set my mind and my wife's mind at rest. Warrender, have you ever seen this gentleman before?" He pointed at Austin, who had risen to his feet, and was standing right under the glare of a tall lamp, the very picture of a hunted man tracked to earth at last.

"Yes, Colonel Reynard, it is the same as I expected."

"The same Austin Gray who was for about a year in the 26th Hussars and who left the regiment and the Service, owing to certain disclosures made through my daughter here," indicating me as he spoke.

"It is the same," said Mr. Warrender quietly.

My father moved a step nearer to Austin. "Sir," he said, speaking with much calmness and dignity, "I do not think that this matter need be further discussed. You will understand without my saying so, that any marriage between you and my daughter is quite impossible."

"Why is it impossible?" demanded Eve, coming forward. "What does all this mean?"

"You heard what Mr. Warrender said . . . You remember the incident of the diamond, star which Nancy here saw . . . But I see you do remember it. This gentleman who does you the honour to wish to marry you, is the hero of that incident."

Eve turned to Austin. "Say this is not true!" she said imperatively.

"I cannot say so," he replied steadily.

She went a step nearer to him and laid her hand on his arm. "Was this what you meant?"

"Yes."

"You had better go home with me to-night," my father went on addressing Eve and ignoring Austin altogether.

"No, I shall stay here," she replied, in the firm tone we all knew so well.

"But what is the use? The sooner everything is finally over the better."

"Nothing can be over," she said in a perfectly unmoved voice.

"What do you mean? You can have no idea of marrying this man!" my father cried passionately.

There was a moment's silence. Then Eve turned and took Austin's hand. "I have married him," she said simply. "And I am quite willing to abide by my choice."

"You have married him!" cried my father, staggering back as if some one had struck him a blow. "When?"

"Yesterday morning," replied Eve steadily.

So this was the meaning of their long absence and their jubilant looks when they returned! And this was the meaning of that one golden thread of triumph which had under-run all the conflict of tempestuous thoughts that for hours had been running riot in his soul.

My father went close to Eve. "My dear child," he said. "You don't understand everything; you don't know half the truth. It is impossible that you can live with this man as his wife. We must try to get the marriage dissolved, and failing that you must be content to come home and try to forget that such wreck and ruin has ever come into your life. Don't you understand that this man is a thief, that he connived to take your favourite brother's life in India, and that Tom would have died by the hand of an assassin had not Heaven itself frustrated his designs? This man cannot deny that his was the hand that pulled the string when Madge's little child nearly died by the hand of this man's . . . But there, I need surely say no more unless it is that when he chanced to come across us in Italy—whether by accident or design, I do not pretend to say—he did not hesitate to pretend an affection for Nancy, which he never felt and by which he only intended to revenge himself still further upon us."

"On my soul, NO," cried Austin, at this moment.

My father turned and looked at him but said never a word. "Eve, I know that this is a most horrible misfortune which has come upon you. My dear, it shall be the object of our lives to——"

But here Eve put up her hand. "Please, stop!" she said, in a strangely fixed voice. "It is no use saying any more. I have quite made up my mind. I have made my bed . . . *and I must lie on it.*"

I don't know what happened next. I turned and fled out into the night, for I could not bear to hear any more. I tore along to the end of the terrace and there I leaned upon the wall overlooking the corner of the park and sobbed out my anguish to the chill summer night. Then a hand was laid on my shoulder and a voice sounded in my ear . . . "Nancy . . . Nancy . . . don't blame me. When I knew it was the same fellow, what else could I do? If I had known that she was married to him, I would have held my tongue for ever, for ever. But how was I to know?"

"Oh, I have known it all for days," I cried, weeping wildly. "I was going to tell

. . . oh, why should it be? What shall I do?"

"But you did not really care for him?" he asked anxiously.

"No, no, of course. But Eve . . . she worships him, worships him. How did Father find out about Tom?"

"I don't know. I think it must have come to him as a possibility and he said it on chance," he replied. "Anyway, the shot struck home."

I turned to go in. The night air was cold and I was shivering. He too turned and walked back beside me. "Nancy," he said half hesitatingly when we got nearly to the window. "I . . I . . wanted to say something to you, and after this awful scene to-night, I hardly know how to say it. It's just this. You'll say that you are glad to see me . . . you'll not send me away . . . I couldn't help all this, you know, and I . . ."

I held my hand out to him. "Let us go in," I said.

THE END.

The Codes Of Hammurabi And Moses
W. W. Davies

QTY

The discovery of the Hammurabi Code is one of the greatest achievements of archaeology, and is of paramount interest, not only to the student of the Bible, but also to all those interested in ancient history...

Religion   **ISBN:** *1-59462-338-4*   **Pages:132**
MSRP $12.95

The Theory of Moral Sentiments
Adam Smith

QTY

This work from 1749. contains original theories of conscience amd moral judgment and it is the foundation for systemof morals.

Philosophy ISBN: *1-59462-777-0*   **Pages:536**
MSRP $19.95

Jessica's First Prayer
Hesba Stretton

QTY

In a screened and secluded corner of one of the many railway-bridges which span the streets of London there could be seen a few years ago, from five o'clock every morning until half past eight, a tidily set-out coffee-stall, consisting of a trestle and board, upon which stood two large tin cans, with a small fire of charcoal burning under each so as to keep the coffee boiling during the early hours of the morning when the work-people were thronging into the city on their way to their daily toil...

Pages:84

Childrens   ISBN: *1-59462-373-2*   *MSRP $9.95*

My Life and Work
Henry Ford

QTY

Henry Ford revolutionized the world with his implementation of mass production for the Model T automobile. Gain valuable business insight into his life and work with his own auto-biography... "We have only started on our development of our country we have not as yet, with all our talk of wonderful progress, done more than scratch the surface. The progress has been wonderful enough but..."

Pages:300

Biographies/   ISBN: *1-59462-198-5*   *MSRP $21.95*

The Art of Cross-Examination
Francis Wellman

QTY

I presume it is the experience of every author, after his first book is published upon an important subject, to be almost overwhelmed with a wealth of ideas and illustrations which could readily have been included in his book, and which to his own mind, at least, seem to make a second edition inevitable. Such certainly was the case with me; and when the first edition had reached its sixth impression in five months, I rejoiced to learn that it seemed to my publishers that the book had met with a sufficiently favorable reception to justify a second and considerably enlarged edition. ...

Reference   **ISBN:** *1-59462-647-2*

Pages:412

MSRP $19.95

On the Duty of Civil Disobedience
Henry David Thoreau

QTY

Thoreau wrote his famous essay, On the Duty of Civil Disobedience, as a protest against an unjust but popular war and the immoral but popular institution of slave-owning. He did more than write—he declined to pay his taxes, and was hauled off to gaol in consequence. Who can say how much this refusal of his hastened the end of the war and of slavery ?

Law   **ISBN:** *1-59462-747-9*

Pages:48

MSRP $7.45

Dream Psychology
Psychoanalysis for Beginners

Sigmund Freud

Dream Psychology Psychoanalysis for Beginners
Sigmund Freud

QTY

Sigmund Freud, born Sigismund Schlomo Freud (May 6, 1856 - September 23, 1939), was a Jewish-Austrian neurologist and psychiatrist who co-founded the psychoanalytic school of psychology. Freud is best known for his theories of the unconscious mind, especially involving the mechanism of repression; his redefinition of sexual desire as mobile and directed towards a wide variety of objects; and his therapeutic techniques, especially his understanding of transference in the therapeutic relationship and the presumed value of dreams as sources of insight into unconscious desires.

Psychology   **ISBN:** *1-59462-905-6*

Pages:196

MSRP $15.45

The Miracle of Right Thought
Orison Swett Marden

QTY

Believe with all of your heart that you will do what you were made to do. When the mind has once formed the habit of holding cheerful, happy, prosperous pictures, it will not be easy to form the opposite habit. It does not matter how improbable or how far away this realization may see, or how dark the prospects may be, if we visualize them as best we can, as vividly as possible, hold tenaciously to them and vigorously struggle to attain them, they will gradually become actualized, realized in the life. But a desire, a longing without endeavor, a yearning abandoned or held indifferently will vanish without realization.

Self Help   **ISBN:** *1-59462-644-8*

Pages:360

MSRP $25.45

www.bookjungle.com *email: sales@bookjungle.com fax: 630-214-0564 mail: Book Jungle PO Box 2226 Champaign, IL 61825*

QTY

The Rosicrucian Cosmo-Conception Mystic Christianity *by Max Heindel*   ISBN: 1-59462-188-8   **$38.95**
The Rosicrucian Cosmo-conception is not dogmatic, neither does it appeal to any other authority than the reason of the student. It is: not controversial, but is: sent forth in the, hope that it may help to clear...   New Age/Religion Pages 646

Abandonment To Divine Providence *by Jean-Pierre de Caussade*   ISBN: 1-59462-228-0   **$25.95**
"The Rev. Jean Pierre de Caussade was one of the most remarkable spiritual writers of the Society of Jesus in France in the 18th Century. His death took place at Toulouse in 1751. His works have gone through many editions and have been republished...   Inspirational/Religion Pages 400

Mental Chemistry *by Charles Haanel*   ISBN: 1-59462-192-6   **$23.95**
Mental Chemistry allows the change of material conditions by combining and appropriately utilizing the power of the mind. Much like applied chemistry creates something new and unique out of careful combinations of chemicals the mastery of mental chemistry...   New Age Pages 354

The Letters of Robert Browning and Elizabeth Barret Barrett 1845-1846 vol II   ISBN: 1-59462-193-4   **$35.95**
by Robert Browning and Elizabeth Barrett   Biographies Pages 596

Gleanings In Genesis (volume I) *by Arthur W. Pink*   ISBN: 1-59462-130-6   **$27.45**
Appropriately has Genesis been termed "the seed plot of the Bible" for in it we have, in germ form, almost all of the great doctrines which are afterwards fully developed in the books of Scripture which follow...   Religion/Inspirational Pages 420

The Master Key *by L. W. de Laurence*   ISBN: 1-59462-001-6   **$30.95**
In no branch of human knowledge has there been a more lively increase of the spirit of research during the past few years than in the study of Psychology, Concentration and Mental Discipline. The requests for authentic lessons in Thought Control, Mental Discipline and...   New Age/Business Pages 422

The Lesser Key Of Solomon Goetia *by L. W. de Laurence*   ISBN: 1-59462-092-X   **$9.95**
This translation of the first book of the "Lernegton" which is now for the first time made accessible to students of Talismanic Magic was done, after careful collation and edition, from numerous Ancient Manuscripts in Hebrew, Latin, and French...   New Age/Occult Pages 92

Rubaiyat Of Omar Khayyam *by Edward Fitzgerald*   ISBN:1-59462-332-5   **$13.95**
Edward Fitzgerald, whom the world has already learned, in spite of his own efforts to remain within the shadow of anonymity, to look upon as one of the rarest poets of the century, was born at Bredfield, in Suffolk, on the 31st of March, 1809. He was the third son of John Purcell...   Music Pages 172

Ancient Law *by Henry Maine*   ISBN: 1-59462-128-4   **$29.95**
The chief object of the following pages is to indicate some of the earliest ideas of mankind, as they are reflected in Ancient Law, and to point out the relation of those ideas to modern thought.   Religion/History Pages 452

Far-Away Stories *by William J. Locke*   ISBN: 1-59462-129-2   **$19.45**
"Good wine needs no bush, but a collection of mixed vintages does. And this book is just such a collection. Some of the stories I do not want to remain buried for ever in the museum files of dead magazine-numbers an author's not unpardonable vanity..."   Fiction Pages 272

Life of David Crockett *by David Crockett*   ISBN: 1-59462-250-7   **$27.45**
"Colonel David Crockett was one of the most remarkable men of the times in which he lived. Born in humble life, but gifted with a strong will, an indomitable courage, and unremitting perseverance...   Biographies/New Age Pages 424

Lip-Reading *by Edward Nitchie*   ISBN: 1-59462-206-X   **$25.95**
Edward B. Nitchie, founder of the New York School for the Hard of Hearing, now the Nitchie School of Lip-Reading, Inc, wrote "LIP-READING Principles and Practice". The development and perfecting of this meritorious work on lip-reading was an undertaking...   How-to Pages 400

A Handbook of Suggestive Therapeutics, Applied Hypnotism, Psychic Science   ISBN: 1-59462-214-0   **$24.95**
by Henry Munro   Health/New Age/Health/Self-help Pages 376

A Doll's House: and Two Other Plays *by Henrik Ibsen*   ISBN: 1-59462-112-8   **$19.95**
Henrik Ibsen created this classic when in revolutionary 1848 Rome. Introducing some striking concepts in playwriting for the realist genre, this play has been studied the world over.   Fiction/Classics/Plays 308

The Light of Asia *by sir Edwin Arnold*   ISBN: 1-59462-204-3   **$13.95**
In this poetic masterpiece, Edwin Arnold describes the life and teachings of Buddha. The man who was to become known as Buddha to the world was born as Prince Gautama of India but he rejected the worldly riches and abandoned the reigns of power when...   Religion/History/Biographies Pages 170

The Complete Works of Guy de Maupassant *by Guy de Maupassant*   ISBN: 1-59462-157-8   **$16.95**
"For days and days, nights and nights, I had dreamed of that first kiss which was to consecrate our engagement, and I knew not on what spot I should put my lips..."   Fiction/Classics Pages 240

The Art of Cross-Examination *by Francis L. Wellman*   ISBN: 1-59462-309-0   **$26.95**
Written by a renowned trial lawyer, Wellman imparts his experience and uses case studies to explain how to use psychology to extract desired information through questioning.   How-to/Science/Reference Pages 408

Answered or Unanswered? *by Louisa Vaughan*   ISBN: 1-59462-248-5   **$10.95**
Miracles of Faith in China   Religion Pages 112

The Edinburgh Lectures on Mental Science (1909) *by Thomas*   ISBN: 1-59462-008-3   **$11.95**
This book contains the substance of a course of lectures recently given by the writer in the Queen Street Hall, Edinburgh. Its purpose is to indicate the Natural Principles governing the relation between Mental Action and Material Conditions...   New Age/Psychology Pages 148

Ayesha *by H. Rider Haggard*   ISBN: 1-59462-301-5   **$24.95**
Verily and indeed it is the unexpected that happens! Probably if there was one person upon the earth from whom the Editor of this, and of a certain previous history, did not expect to hear again...   Classics Pages 380

Ayala's Angel *by Anthony Trollope*   ISBN: 1-59462-352-X   **$29.95**
The two girls were both pretty, but Lucy who was twenty-one who supposed to be simple and comparatively unattractive, whereas Ayala was credited, as her Bombwhat romantic name might show, with poetic charm and a taste for romance. Ayala when her father died was nineteen...   Fiction Pages 484

The American Commonwealth *by James Bryce*   ISBN: 1-59462-286-8   **$34.45**
An interpretation of American democratic political theory. It examines political mechanics and society from the perspective of Scotsman James Bryce   Politics Pages 572

Stories of the Pilgrims *by Margaret P. Pumphrey*   ISBN: 1-59462-116-0   **$17.95**
This book explores pilgrims religious oppression in England as well as their escape to Holland and eventual crossing to America on the Mayflower, and their early days in New England...   History Pages 268

www.bookjungle.com *email: sales@bookjungle.com fax: 630-214-0564 mail: Book Jungle PO Box 2226 Champaign, IL 61825*

QTY

The Fasting Cure *by Sinclair Upton*   ISBN: *1-59462-222-1* **$13.95**
In the Cosmopolitan Magazine for May, 1910, and in the Contemporary Review (London) for April, 1910, I published an article dealing with my experiences in fasting. I have written a great many magazine articles, but never one which attracted so much attention... New Age/Self Help/Health Pages 164

Hebrew Astrology *by Sepharial*   ISBN: *1-59462-308-2* **$13.45**
In these days of advanced thinking it is a matter of common observation that we have left many of the old landmarks behind and that we are now pressing forward to greater heights and to a wider horizon than that which represented the mind-content of our progenitors...   Astrology Pages 144

Thought Vibration or The Law of Attraction in the Thought World   ISBN: *1-59462-127-6* **$12.95**
by William Walker Atkinson   Psychology/Religion Pages 144

Optimism *by Helen Keller*   ISBN: *1-59462-108-X* **$15.95**
Helen Keller was blind, deaf, and mute since 19 months old, yet famously learned how to overcome these handicaps, communicate with the world, and spread her lectures promoting optimism. An inspiring read for everyone...   Biographies/Inspirational Pages 84

Sara Crewe *by Frances Burnett*   ISBN: *1-59462-360-0*   **$9.45**
In the first place, Miss Minchin lived in London. Her home was a large, dull, tall one, in a large, dull square, where all the houses were alike, and all the sparrows were alike, and where all the door-knockers made the same heavy sound...   Childrens/Classic Pages 88

The Autobiography of Benjamin Franklin *by Benjamin Franklin*   ISBN: *1-59462-135-7* **$24.95**
The Autobiography of Benjamin Franklin has probably been more extensively read than any other American historical work, and no other book of its kind has had such ups and downs of fortune. Franklin lived for many years in England, where he was agent...   Biographies/History Pages 332

Name	
Email	
Telephone	
Address	
City, State ZIP	

☐ **Credit Card**   ☐ **Check / Money Order**

Credit Card Number	
Expiration Date	
Signature	

Please Mail to: *Book Jungle*
PO Box 2226
Champaign, IL 61825
or Fax to: *630-214-0564*

ORDERING INFORMATION

web*: www.bookjungle.com*
email*: sales@bookjungle.com*
fax*: 630-214-0564*
mail*: Book Jungle PO Box 2226 Champaign, IL 61825*
or PayPal *to sales@bookjungle.com*

Please contact us for bulk discounts

DIRECT-ORDER TERMS

**20% Discount if You Order
Two or More Books**
Free Domestic Shipping!
Accepted: Master Card, Visa,
Discover, American Express

www.ingramcontent.com/pod-product-compliance
Lightning Source LLC
Chambersburg PA
CBHW080908020726
47502CB00008B/2389